Ru

KIM THÚY

Ru

A Novel

Translated from the French by SHEILA FISCHMAN

BLOOMSBURY
NEW YORK · LONDON · NEW DELHI · SYDNEY

Published by arrangement with Random House Canada, an imprint of the
Knopf Random Canada Publishing Group which is a division of Random
House of Canada Limited.

Published by Bloomsbury USA, New York

All papers used by Bloomsbury USA are natural, recyclable products made
from wood grown in well-managed forests. The manufacturing processes
conform to the environmental regulations of the country of origin.

LIBRARY OF CONGRESS CATALOGING-IN-PUBLICATION DATA HAS BEEN APPLIED
FOR.

ISBN: 978-1-60819-898-6

Originally published in French in Canada as *Ru* by Éditions Libre
Expression, Montreal, in 2009
First published in English by Random House Canada, a division of Random
House of Canada Limited, Toronto, and simultaneously in the United
Kingdom by The Clerkenwell Press, a division of Profile Books Limited,
London, in 2012

First U.S. Edition 2012

1 3 5 7 9 10 8 6 4 2

Book design by CS Richardson
Printed in the U.S.A.

In French, *ru* means a small stream and, figuratively, a flow, a discharge—of tears, of blood, of money. In Vietnamese, *ru* means a lullaby, to lull.

I came into the world during the Tet Offensive, in the early days of the Year of the Monkey, when the long chains of firecrackers draped in front of houses exploded polyphonically along with the sound of machine guns.

I first saw the light of day in Saigon, where firecrackers, fragmented into a thousand shreds, coloured the ground red like the petals of cherry blossoms or like the blood of the two million soldiers deployed and scattered throughout the villages and cities of a Vietnam that had been ripped in two.

I was born in the shadow of skies adorned with fireworks, decorated with garlands of light, shot through with rockets and missiles. The purpose of my birth was to replace lives that had been lost. My life's duty was to prolong that of my mother.

My name is Nguyễn An Tịnh, my mother's name is Nguyễn An Tĩnh. My name is simply a variation on hers because a single dot under the *i* differentiates, distinguishes, dissociates me from her. I was an extension of her, even in the meaning of my name. In Vietnamese, hers means "peaceful environment" and mine "peaceful interior." With those almost interchangeable names, my mother confirmed that I was the sequel to her, that I would continue her story.

The History of Vietnam, written with a capital H, thwarted my mother's plans. History flung the accents on our names into the water when it took us across the Gulf of Siam thirty years ago. It also stripped our names of their meaning, reducing them to sounds at once strange, and strange to the French language. In particular, when I was ten years old it ended my role as an extension of my mother.

B ecause of our exile, my children have never been
extensions of me, of my history. Their names
are Pascal and Henri, and they don't look like me.
They have hair that's lighter in colour than mine,
white skin, thick eyelashes. I did not experience the
natural feelings of motherhood I'd expected when
they were clamped onto my breasts at 3 a.m., in the
middle of the night. The maternal instinct came to
me much later, over the course of sleepless nights,
dirty diapers, unexpected smiles, sudden delights.

Only then did I understand the love of the mother
sitting across from me in the hold of our boat,
the head of the baby in her arms covered with
foul-smelling scabies. That image was before my
eyes for days and maybe nights as well. The small
bulb hanging from a wire attached to a rusty nail
spread a feeble, unchanging light. Deep inside the
boat there was no distinction between day and night.
The constant illumination protected us from the
vastness of the sea and the sky all around us.
The people sitting on deck told us there was no
boundary between the blue of the sky and the blue
of the sea. No one knew if we were heading for
the heavens or plunging into the water's depths.
Heaven and hell embraced in the belly of our
boat. Heaven promised a turning point in our lives,
a new future, a new history. Hell, though, displayed
our fears: fear of pirates, fear of starvation, fear
of poisoning by biscuits soaked in motor oil, fear of

running out of water, fear of being unable to stand up, fear of having to urinate in the red pot that was passed from hand to hand, fear that the scabies on the baby's head was contagious, fear of never again setting foot on solid ground, fear of never again seeing the faces of our parents, who were sitting in the darkness surrounded by two hundred people.

B efore our boat had weighed anchor in the middle of the night on the shores of Rach Gia, most of the passengers had just one fear: fear of the Communists, the reason for their flight. But as soon as the vessel was surrounded, encircled by the uniform blue horizon, fear was transformed into a hundred-faced monster who sawed off our legs and kept us from feeling the stiffness in our immobilized muscles. We were frozen in fear, by fear. We no longer closed our eyes when the scabious little boy's pee sprayed us. We no longer pinched our noses against our neighbours' vomit. We were numb, imprisoned by the shoulders of some, the legs of others, the fear of everyone. We were paralyzed.

The story of the little girl who was swallowed up by the sea after she'd lost her footing while walking along the edge spread through the foul-smelling belly of the boat like an anaesthetic or laughing gas, transforming the single bulb into a polar star and the biscuits soaked in motor oil into butter cookies. The taste of oil in our throats, on our tongues, in our heads sent us to sleep to the rhythm of the lullaby sung by the woman beside me.

My father had made plans, should our family be captured by Communists or pirates, to put us to sleep forever, like Sleeping Beauty, with cyanide pills. For a long time afterwards, I wanted to ask why he hadn't thought of letting us choose, why he would have taken away our possibility of survival.

I stopped asking myself that question when I became a mother, when Dr. Vinh, a highly regarded surgeon in Saigon, told me how he had put his five children, one after the other, from the boy of twelve to the little girl of five, alone, on five different boats, at five different times, to send them off to sea, far from the charges of the Communist authorities that hung over him. He was certain he would die in prison because he'd been accused of killing some Communist comrades by operating on them, even if they'd never set foot in his hospital. He hoped to save one, maybe two of his children by launching them in this fashion onto the sea. I met Dr. Vinh on the church steps, which he cleared of snow in the winter and swept in the summer to thank the priest who had acted as father to his children, bringing up all five, one after the other, until they were grown, until the doctor got out of prison.

I didn't cry out and I didn't weep when I was told that my son Henri was a prisoner in his own world, when it was confirmed that he is one of those children who don't hear us, don't speak to us, even though they're neither deaf nor mute. He is also one of those children we must love from a distance, neither touching, nor kissing, nor smiling at them because every one of their senses would be assaulted by the odour of our skin, by the intensity of our voices, the texture of our hair, the throbbing of our hearts. Probably he'll never call me *maman* lovingly, even if he can pronounce the word *poire* with all the roundness and sensuality of the *oi* sound. He will never understand why I cried when he smiled for the first time. He won't know that, thanks to him, every spark of joy has become a blessing and that I will keep waging war against autism, even if I know already that it's invincible.

Already, I am defeated, stripped bare, beaten down.

When I saw my first snowbanks through the porthole of the plane at Mirabel Airport, then too I felt naked, if not stripped bare. In spite of my short-sleeved orange pullover purchased at the refugee camp in Malaysia before we left for Canada, in spite of my loose-knit brown sweater made by Vietnamese women, I was naked. Several of us on the plane made a dash for the windows, our mouths agape, our expressions stunned. After such a long time in places without light, a landscape so white, so virginal could only dazzle us, blind us, intoxicate us.

I was as surprised by all the unfamiliar sounds that greeted us as by the size of the ice sculpture watching over a table covered with canapés, hors d'oeuvre, tasty morsels, each more colourful than the last. I recognized none of the dishes, yet I knew that this was a place of delights, an idyllic land. I was like my son Henri: unable to talk or to listen, even though I was neither deaf nor mute. I now had no points of reference, no tools to allow me to dream, to project myself into the future, to be able to experience the present, in the present.

M y first teacher in Canada walked with us, the seven youngest in the group of Vietnamese, across the bridge that led to the present. She watched over our transplantation with all the sensitivity of a mother for her premature baby. We were hypnotized by the slow and reassuring swaying of her shapely hips, her round and generous behind. Like a mother duck, she walked ahead of us, asking us to follow her to the haven where we would be children again, simply children, surrounded by colours, drawings, trivia. I will be forever grateful to her for giving me my first desire as an immigrant: to be able to sway my bum the way she did. Not one of the Vietnamese in our group possessed such opulence, such generosity, such nonchalance in her curves. We were all angular, bony, hard. And so when she bent down to me, placing her hands on mine to tell me, "My name is Marie-France, what's yours?" I repeated each of her syllables without blinking, without needing to understand, because I was lulled by a cloud of coolness, of lightness, of sweet perfume. I hadn't understood a word she'd said, only the melody of her voice, but it was enough. More than enough.

When I got home, I repeated the same sequence of sounds to my parents: "My name is Marie-France, what's yours?" They asked me if I'd changed my name. It was at that split second that my present reality caught up to me, when the deafness and muteness of the moment erased my dreams and thus the power to look ahead, to look far ahead.

My parents, though they already spoke French, could not look far ahead either, for they'd been expelled from the Introduction to French course, that is, struck off the list of people who would receive an allowance of forty dollars a week. They were overqualified for the course but underqualified for everything else. Unable to look ahead of themselves, they looked ahead of us, for us, their children.

For us, they didn't see the blackboards they wiped clean, the school toilets they scrubbed, the imperial rolls they delivered. They saw only what lay ahead. And so to make progress my brothers and I followed where their eyes led us. I met parents whose gaze had been extinguished, some beneath the weight of a pirate's body, others during the all too many years of Communist re-education camps—not the war camps during the war, but the peacetime camps after the war.

As a child, I thought that war and peace were opposites. Yet I lived in peace when Vietnam was in flames and I didn't experience war until Vietnam had laid down its weapons. I believe that war and peace are actually friends, who mock us. They treat us like enemies when it suits them, with no concern for the definition or the role we give them. Perhaps, then, we shouldn't take too much stock in the appearance of one or the other to decide our views. I was lucky enough to have parents who were able to hold their gaze steady, no matter the mood of the moment. My mother often recited the proverb that was written on the blackboard of her eighth-grade class in Saigon: Đời là chiến trận, nếu buồn là thua. *Life is a struggle in which sorrow leads to defeat.*

My mother waged her first battles later, without sorrow. She went to work for the first time at the age of thirty-four, first as a cleaning lady, then at jobs in plants, factories, restaurants. Before, in the life that she had lost, she was the eldest daughter of her prefect father. All she did was settle arguments between the French-food chef and the Vietnamese-food chef in the family courtyard. Or she assumed the role of judge in the secret love affairs between maids and menservants. Otherwise, she spent her afternoons doing her hair, applying her makeup, getting dressed to accompany my father to social events. Thanks to the extravagant life she lived, she could dream all the dreams she wanted, especially those she dreamed for us. She was preparing my brothers and me to become musicians, scientists, politicians, athletes, artists and polyglots, all at the same time.

However, far from us, blood still flowed and bombs still fell, so she taught us to get down on our knees like the servants. Every day, she made me wash four tiles on the floor and clean twenty sprouted beans by removing their roots one by one. She was preparing us for the collapse. She was right to do so, because very soon we no longer had a floor beneath our feet.

During our first nights as refugees in Malaysia, we slept right on the red earth, without a floor. The Red Cross had built refugee camps in the countries adjoining Vietnam to receive the boat people—those who had survived the sea journey. The others, those who'd gone down during the crossing, had no names. They died anonymously. We were among those who had been lucky enough to wash up on dry land. We felt blessed to be among the two thousand refugees in a camp that was intended to hold two hundred.

W e built a cabin on piles in an out-of-the-way part of the camp, on the side of a hill. For weeks, twenty-five members of five families working together, in secret, felled some trees in the nearby woods, then planted them in the soft clay soil, attached them to six plywood panels to make a large floor, and covered the frame with a canvas of electric blue, plastic blue, toy blue. We had the good fortune to find enough burlap and nylon rice bags to surround the four sides of our cabin, as well as the three sides of our shared bathroom. Together, the two structures resembled a museum installation by a contemporary artist. At night, we slept pressed so close together that we were never cold, even without a blanket. During the day, the heat absorbed by the blue plastic made the air in our cabin suffocating. On rainy days and nights, the water came in through holes pierced by the leaves, twigs and stems that we'd added to cool it down.

If a choreographer had been underneath the plastic sheet on a rainy day or night, he would certainly have reproduced the scene: twenty-five people, short and tall, on their feet, each holding a tin can to collect the water that dripped off the roof, sometimes in torrents, sometimes drop by drop. If a musician had been there, he would have heard the orchestration of all that water striking the sides of the tins. If a filmmaker had been there, he would have captured the beauty of the silent and spontaneous complicity between wretched people. But there was only us, standing on a floor that was slowly sinking into the clay. After three months it tilted so severely to one side that we all had to find new positions so sleeping women and children wouldn't slip onto the plump bellies of their neighbours.

In spite of all those nights when our dreams spilled onto the sloping floor, my mother still had high hopes for our future. She'd found an accomplice. He was young and certainly naive because he dared to flaunt joy and light-heartedness in the midst of our dull and empty daily lives. Together, he and my mother started an English class. We spent whole mornings with him, repeating words we didn't understand. But we all showed up because he was able to raise the sky and give us a glimpse of a new horizon, far from the gaping holes filled with the excrement of the camp's two thousand people. Without his face, we could never have imagined a horizon without flies, worms and nauseating smells. Without his face, we couldn't have imagined that someday we would no longer eat rotting fish flung down late every afternoon when rations were handed out. Without his face, we would certainly have lost the desire to reach out our hands and catch our dreams.

Unfortunately, from all the mornings with this impromptu English teacher, I remembered only one sentence: *My boat number is KG0338.* It turned out to be totally useless because I never had a chance to say it, not even during the medical examination by the Canadian delegation. The doctor on call didn't speak a word to me. He tugged the elastic of my pants to confirm my sex instead of asking, *Boy or girl?* I also knew those two words. The appearance of a ten-year-old boy and a ten-year-old girl must have been much the same, because of our scrawniness. And time was short: there were so many of us on the other side of the door. It was terribly hot in the small examining room with its windows open onto a noisy alley where hundreds of water buckets collided at the pump. We were covered with scabies and lice and we all looked lost, beyond our depth.

In any case, I spoke very little, sometimes not at all. Throughout my early childhood, my cousin Sao Mai always spoke on my behalf because I was her shadow: the same age, the same class, the same sex, but her face was on the bright side and mine on the side of darkness, shadow, silence.

M y mother wanted me to talk, to learn French as fast as possible, English too, because my mother tongue had become not exactly insufficient, but useless. Starting in my second year in Quebec, she sent me to a military garrison of anglophone cadets. It was a way that I could learn English for free, she told me. But she was wrong, it wasn't free. I paid for it, dearly. There were around forty cadets, all of them tall, bursting with energy and, above all, teenagers. They took themselves seriously when inspecting in minute detail the fold of a collar, the angle of a beret, the shine of a boot. The oldest ones yelled at the youngest. They played at war, at the absurd, without understanding. And I didn't understand them.
Nor did I understand why the name of the cadet next to me was repeated in a loop by our superior. Maybe he wanted me to remember the name of that teenage boy who was twice my height. My first conversation in English started with me saying to him at the end of the session: "Bye, Asshole."

My mother often put me in situations of extreme shame. Once, she asked me to go and buy sugar at the grocery store just below our first apartment. I went but found no sugar. My mother sent me back and even locked the door behind me: "Don't come back without the sugar!" She had forgotten that I was a deaf-mute. I sat on the grocery store steps until it closed, until the grocer took me by the hand and led me to the bag of sugar. He had understood, even if to me the word *sugar* was bitter.

For a long time, I thought my mother enjoyed constantly pushing me right to the edge. When I had my own children, I finally understood that I should have seen her behind the locked door, eyes pressed against the peephole; I should have heard her talking on the phone to the grocer when I was sitting on the steps in tears. I also understood later that my mother certainly had dreams for me, but above all she'd given me tools so that I could put down roots, so that I could dream.

The town of Granby was the warm belly that sheltered us during our first year in Canada. The locals cosseted us one by one. The pupils in my grade school lined up to invite us home for lunch so that each of our noon hours was reserved by a family.

And every time, we went back to school with nearly empty stomachs because we didn't know how to use a fork to eat rice that wasn't sticky. We didn't know how to tell them that this food was strange to us, that they really didn't have to go to every grocery store in search of the last box of Minute Rice. We could neither talk to nor understand them. But that wasn't the main thing. There was generosity and gratitude in every grain of the rice left on our plates. To this day I still wonder whether words might have tainted those moments of grace. And whether feelings are sometimes understood better in silence, like the one that existed between Claudette and Monsieur Kiet. Their first moments together were wordless, yet Monsieur Kiet agreed to put his baby into Claudette's arms without questioning: a baby, his baby, whom he'd found on the shore after his boat had capsized in an especially greedy wave. He had not found his wife, only his son, who was experiencing a second birth without his mother. Claudette stretched out her arms to them and kept them with her for days, for months, for years.

J ohanne held out her hand to me in the same way.
She liked me even though I wore a tuque with a
McDonald's logo, even though I travelled hidden in
a cube van with fifty other Vietnamese to work in
fields around the Eastern Townships after school.
Johanne wanted me to go to a private secondary
school with her the following year. Yet she knew
that I waited every afternoon in the yard of that very
school for the farmers' trucks that would take us to
work illegally in the fields, earning a few dollars in
exchange for the sacks of beans we picked.

Johanne also took me to the movies, even though
I was wearing a shirt bought on sale for eighty-eight
cents, with a hole near one of the seams. After the
film *Fame* she taught me how to sing the theme
song in English, "I sing the body electric," although
I didn't understand the words, or her conversations
with her sister and her parents around their fireplace.
It was Johanne too who picked me up after my first
falls when we went ice skating, who applauded
and shouted my name in the crowd when Serge,
a classmate three times my size, took me in his arms
along with the football and scored a touchdown.

I wonder if I haven't invented her, that friend
of mine. I've met many people who believe in God,
but what I believe in is angels, and Johanne was an
angel. She was one of an army of them who'd been
parachuted into town to give us shock treatment.
By the dozen they showed up at our doors to give us

warm clothes, toys, invitations, dreams. I often
felt there wasn't enough space inside us to receive
everything we were offered, to catch all the smiles
that came our way. How could we visit the Granby
zoo more than twice each weekend? How could we
appreciate a camping trip to the countryside? How
to savour an omelette with maple syrup?

I have a photo of my father being embraced by
our sponsors, a family of volunteers to whom
we'd been assigned. They spent their Sundays taking
us to flea markets. They negotiated fiercely on our
behalf so we could buy mattresses, dishes, beds,
sofas—in short, the basics—with our three-hundred-
dollar government allowance meant to furnish our
first home in Quebec. One of the vendors threw in
a red cowl-necked sweater for my father. He wore
it proudly every day of our first spring in Quebec.
Today, his broad smile in the photo from that time
manages to make us forget that it was a woman's
sweater, nipped in at the waist. Sometimes it's best
not to know everything.

Of course, there were times when we'd have liked
to know more. To know, for instance, that in our old
mattresses there were fleas. But those details don't
matter because they don't show in the pictures. In any
case, we thought we were immunized against stings,
that no flea could pierce our skin bronzed by the
Malaysian sun. In fact, the cold winds and hot baths
had purified us, making the bites unbearable and the
itches bloody.

We threw out the mattresses without telling our
sponsors. We didn't want them to be disappointed,
because they'd given us their hearts, their time.
We appreciated their generosity, but not sufficiently:
we did not yet know the cost of time, its fair market
value, its tremendous scarcity.

For a whole year, Granby represented heaven
on earth. I couldn't imagine a better place in
the world, even if we were being eaten alive by flies,
just as in the refugee camp. A local botanist took
us children to swamps where cattails grew in the
thousands, to show us the insects. He didn't know
that we'd rubbed shoulders with flies in the refugee
camps for months. They clung to the branches of a
dead tree near the septic tanks, next to our cabin.
They positioned themselves around the branches like
the berries of a pepper plant or currants. They were
so numerous, so enormous, that they didn't need to
fly to be in front of our eyes, in our lives. We didn't
need to be silent to hear them. Now our botanist
guide whispered to us to listen to their droning,
to try to understand them.

I know the sound of flies by heart. I just have to close my eyes to hear them buzzing around me again, because for months I had to crouch down above a gigantic pit filled to the brim with excrement, in the blazing sun of Malaysia. I had to look at the indescribable brown colour without blinking so that I wouldn't slip on the two planks behind the door of one of the sixteen cabins every time I set foot there. I had to keep my balance, avoid fainting when my stools or those from the next cabin splattered. At those moments I escaped by listening to the humming of flies. Once, I lost my slipper between the planks after I'd moved my foot too quickly. It fell into the cesspit without sinking, floating there like a boat cast adrift.

I went barefoot for days, waiting for my mother to find an orphan slipper belonging to another child who'd also lost one. I walked directly on the clay soil where maggots had been crawling a week before. With every heavy rainfall they emerged from the cesspit in the hundreds of thousands, as if summoned by a messiah. They all headed for the side of our hill and climbed without ever tiring, without ever falling. They crawled up to our feet, all to the same rhythm, transforming the red clay soil into an undulating white carpet. There were so many that we gave up before we'd even started to fight. They became invincible, we became vulnerable. We let them extend their territory until the rains stopped, when they became vulnerable in turn.

When the Communists entered Saigon, my family handed over half of our property because we'd become vulnerable. A brick wall was erected to establish two addresses: one for us and one for the local police station.

A year later, the authorities from the new Communist administration arrived to clean out our half of the house, to clean us out. Inspectors came to our courtyard with no warning, no authorization, no reason. They asked all those present to gather in the living room. My parents were out, so the inspectors waited for them, sitting on the edges of art deco chairs, their backs straight, without once touching the two white linen squares covered with fine embroidery that adorned the armrests. My mother was the first to appear behind the wrought iron glass door. She had on her white pleated miniskirt and her running shoes. Behind her, my father was dragging tennis rackets, his face still covered in sweat. The inspectors' surprise visit had thrown us into the present while we were still savouring the last moments of the past. All the adults in the household were ordered to stay in the living room while the inspectors started making their inventory.

We children could follow them from floor to floor, from room to room. They sealed chests of drawers, wardrobes, dressing tables, safes. They even sealed the big chests of drawers filled with the brassieres of my grandmother and her six daughters, without describing the contents. It seemed to me then that the young inspector was embarrassed at the thought of all those round-breasted girls in the living room, dressed in fine lace imported from Paris. I also thought that he was leaving the paper blank, with no description of the wardrobe's contents, because he was too overwhelmed by desire to write without trembling. But I was wrong: he had no idea what brassieres were for. In his opinion they looked like his mother's coffee filters, made of cloth sewn around a metal ring, the twisted end of which served as a handle.

At the foot of the Long Biên Bridge that crosses the Red River in Hanoi, every night his mother would fill her coffee filter then dip it into her aluminum coffee pot to make a few cups that she'd sell to passersby. In the winter, she placed glasses containing barely three sips into a bowl filled with hot water to keep them warm during conversations between the men sitting on benches raised just a bit above the ground. Her customers spotted her by the flame of her tiny oil lamp sitting on the tiny work table, next to three cigarettes displayed on a plate. Every morning, the young inspector, still a child, woke up with the oft-mended brown cloth coffee filter, sometimes still wet and hanging from a nail above his head. I heard him talking with the other inspectors in a corner of the staircase. He didn't understand why my family had so many coffee filters filed away in drawers lined with tissue paper. And why were they double? Was it because we always drink coffee with a friend?

The young inspector had been marching in the jungle since the age of twelve to free South Vietnam from the "hairy hands" of the Americans. He had slept in underground tunnels, spent days at a time in a pond, under a water lily, seen the bodies of comrades sacrificed to prevent cannons from sliding, lived through nights of malaria amidst the sound of helicopters and explosions. Aside from his mother's teeth lacquered jet black, he had forgotten his parents' faces. How could he have guessed, then, what a brassiere was for? In the jungle, boys and girls had exactly the same possessions: a green helmet, sandals made from strips of worn-out tires, a uniform, and a black and white checked scarf. An inventory of their belongings took three seconds, unlike ours, which lasted for a year. We had to share our space by taking ten of those girl and boy soldier-inspectors into our home. We gave them one floor of the house. Each of us lived in our own corner, avoiding contact except during the daily searches, when we were obliged to stand face to face with them. They needed to be sure that we had only the essentials, like them.

One day our ten roomers dragged us to their bathroom, accusing us of stealing a fish they'd been given for their evening meal. They pointed to the toilet bowl and explained to us that the fish had been there that morning, hale and hearty. What had become of it?

Thanks to that fish, we were able to establish communication. Later on, my father corrupted them by having them listen to music on the sly. I sat underneath the piano, in the shadows, watching tears roll down their cheeks, where the horrors of History, without hesitation, had carved grooves. After that, we no longer knew if they were enemies or victims, if we loved or hated them, if we feared or pitied them. And they no longer knew if they had freed us from the Americans or, on the contrary, if we had freed them from the jungle of Vietnam.

Very quickly, though, the music that had accorded them a kind of freedom found itself in a fire, on the rooftop terrace of the house. They had received an order to burn the books, songs, films—everything that betrayed the image of those men and women with muscular arms holding aloft their pitchforks, their hammers and their flag, red with a yellow star. Very quickly, they filled the sky with smoke, once more.

What became of those soldiers? Much has changed since the brick wall was put up between us and the Communists. I went back to Vietnam to work with those who had caused the wall to be built, who'd imagined it as a tool to break hundreds of thousands of lives, perhaps even millions. There had been reversals, of course, since the tanks first rolled down the street that ran past our house in 1975. Since then, I had even learned the Communist vocabulary of our former assailants because the Berlin Wall fell, because the Iron Curtain was raised, because I am still too young to be weighed down by the past. Only, there will never be a brick wall in my house. I still don't share the love for brick walls of the people around me. They claim that bricks make a room warm.

The day I started my job in Hanoi, I walked past a tiny room that opened onto the street. Inside, a man and a woman were arranging bricks into a low wall that divided the room in two.

The wall got higher day by day, until it reached the ceiling. My secretary told me that it was because of two brothers who didn't want to live under the same roof. The mother had been helpless against this separation, perhaps because she herself had erected similar walls some thirty years earlier between victors and vanquished. She died during my three-year stay in Hanoi. By way of legacy, to the older child she left the fan without a switch, to the younger the switch without the fan.

It's true that the brick wall between those two
brothers can't be compared to the one that existed
between my family and the Communist soldiers,
nor do these two walls carry the same history as do
old Québécois houses—each wall has its own story. It
is thanks to that distance that I've been able to
share meals with people who were the right arm
and the left arm of Ho Chi Minh without seeing the
rancour hovering, without seeing women on a train
holding old Guigoz powdered milk cans in their
hands as if they were jars of magic potion. For the
men shut away in re-education camps, it *was* a magic
potion, even if the cans held only browned meat
(*thịt chà bông*): a kilo of roasted pork shredded fibre
by fibre, dried all night over the embers, salted,
then salted again with nước mắm obtained after
two days of waiting in line, two days of hope and
despair. The women lavished devotion on those
filaments of pork, even if they weren't sure of finding
their children's father in the camp they were setting
off to visit, not knowing if he was dead or alive,
wounded or sick. In memory of those women,
I cook that browned meat for my sons now and
then, to preserve, to repeat, those gestures of love.

Love, as my son Pascal knows it, is defined by
the number of hearts drawn on a card or
by how many stories about dragons are told by
flashlight under a down-filled comforter. I have to
wait a few more years till I can report to him that in
other times, other places, parents showed their love
by willingly abandoning their children, like the
parents of Tom Thumb. Similarly, the mother who
made me glide on the water with the help of her long
stick, surrounded by the high mountain peaks of
Hoa Lư, wanted to give up her daughter, pass her
to me. That mother wanted me to replace her.
She preferred to cry over her child's absence rather
than watch her running after tourists to sell them
the tablecloths she had embroidered. I was a young
girl then. In the midst of those rocky mountains,
I saw only a majestic landscape in place of that
mother's infinite love. There are nights when I run
along the long strips of earth next to the buffalo
to call her back, to take her daughter's hand in mine.

I am waiting till Pascal is a few years older before
I make the connection between the story of
the mother from Hoa Lư and Tom Thumb. In the
meantime, I tell him the story of the pig that travelled
in a coffin to get through the surveillance posts
between the countryside and the towns. He likes
to hear me imitate the crying women in the funeral
procession who threw themselves body and soul onto
the long wooden box, wailing, while the farmers,
dressed all in white with bands around their heads,
tried to hold them back, to console them in front
of the inspectors who were too accustomed to death.
Once they got back to town, behind the closed doors
of an ever-changing secret address, the farmers
turned the pig over to the butcher, who cut it into
pieces. The merchants would then tie those around
their legs and waists to transport them to the black
market, to families, to us.

I tell Pascal these stories to keep alive the memory
of a slice of history that will never be taught in
any school.

I remember some students in my high school who complained about the compulsory history classes. Young as we were, we didn't realize that the course was a privilege only countries at peace can afford. Elsewhere, people are too preoccupied by their day-to-day survival to take the time to write their collective history. If I hadn't lived in the majestic silence of great frozen lakes, in the humdrum everyday life of peace, where love is celebrated with balloons, confetti, chocolates, I would probably never have noticed the old woman who lived near my great-grandfather's grave in the Mekong Delta. She was very old, so old that the sweat ran down her wrinkles like a brook that traces a furrow in the earth. Her back was hunched, so hunched that she had to go down staircases backwards so as not to lose her balance and fall headfirst. How many grains of rice had she planted? How long had she spent with her feet in the mud? How many suns had she watched set over her rice fields? How many dreams had she set aside only to find herself bent in two, thirty years, forty years later?

We often forget about the existence of all those women who carried Vietnam on their backs while their husbands and sons carried weapons on theirs. We forget them because under their cone-shaped hats they did not look up at the sky. They waited only for the sun to set on them so they could faint instead of falling asleep. Had they taken the time to let sleep

come, they would have imagined their sons blown
into a thousand pieces or the bodies of their husbands
drifting along a river like flotsam. American slaves
were able to sing about their sorrow in the cotton
fields. Those women let their sadness grow in the
chambers of their hearts. They were so weighed
down by all their grief that they couldn't pull
themselves up, couldn't straighten their hunched
backs, bowed under the weight of their sorrow.
When the men emerged from the jungle and started
to walk again along the earthen dikes around their
rice fields, the women continued to bear the weight
of Vietnam's inaudible history on their backs.
Very often they passed away under that weight,
in silence.

One of those women, whom I knew, died when
she lost her footing in the toilet, perched above a pond
full of bullheads. Her plastic slippers slid. Anyone
watching her at that moment would have seen her
cone-shaped hat disappear behind the four panels
that barely hid her crouching body, surrounding her
without protecting her. She died in the family's septic
tank, her head plunging into a hole full of excrement
between two planks, behind her hut, surrounded by
smooth-skinned, yellow-fleshed bullheads, without
scales, without memory.

After the old lady died, I would go every Sunday to a lotus pond in a suburb of Hanoi where there were always two or three women with bent backs and trembling hands, sitting in a small round boat, using a stick to move across the water and drop tea leaves into open lotus blossoms. They would come back the next day to collect them one by one before the petals faded, after the captive tea leaves had absorbed the scent of the pistils during the night. They told me that every one of those tea leaves preserved the soul of the short-lived flowers.

P hotos could not preserve the soul of our first
Christmas trees. Those branches gathered in
the woods of suburban Montreal, stuck in the rim
of a spare tire covered with a white sheet, seem bare
and lacking in magic, but in reality they were much
prettier than the eight-foot-tall spruce trees we
have nowadays.

My parents often remind my brothers and me
that they won't have any money for us to inherit,
but I think they've already passed on to us the wealth
of their memories, allowing us to grasp the beauty of
a flowering wisteria, the delicacy of a word, the power
of wonder. Even more, they've given us feet for
walking to our dreams, to infinity. Which may be
enough baggage to continue our journey on our own.
Otherwise, we would pointlessly clutter our path
with possessions to transport, to insure, to take care of.

A Vietnamese saying has it that "Only those with
long hair are afraid, for no one can pull the hair of
those who have none." And so I try as much as
possible to acquire only those things that don't
extend beyond the limits of my body.

In any case, since our escape by boat, we learned
how to travel very light. The gentleman seated
next to my uncle in the hold had no luggage, not even
a small bag with warm clothes like us. He had on
everything he owned. Swimming trunks, shorts,
pants, T-shirt, shirt and sweater, and the rest was
in his orifices: diamonds embedded in his molars,
gold on his teeth and American dollars stuffed in
his anus. Once we were at sea, we saw women open
their sanitary napkins to take out the American
dollars impeccably folded lengthwise in three.

As for me, I had an acrylic bracelet, pink like
the gums of the dental plate it had been made from,
filled with diamonds. My parents had also
put diamonds in the collars of my brothers' shirts.
But we had no gold in our teeth because it was
forbidden to touch the teeth of my mother's children.
She often told us that teeth and hair are the roots,
maybe even the fundamental source, of a person.
My mother wanted our teeth to be perfect.

That's why even in a refugee camp she was able
to find a pair of dental pliers to pull out our loose
baby teeth. She waved each extracted tooth in
front of us under the blazing Malaysian sun.
Those blood-stained teeth were proudly displayed
against the backdrop of a fine sandy beach and a
barbed-wire fence. My mother told me it would be
possible to enlarge my eyes and maybe even to fix
my ears, which stuck out too much. She couldn't

fix the other structural imperfections of my face,
though, so at least I should have flawless teeth and
above all not trade them for diamonds. She also
knew that if our boat had been intercepted by
Thai pirates, the gold teeth and those that were
filled with diamonds would have been pulled out.

The police were ordered to allow all boats carrying Vietnamese of Chinese background to leave "in secret." The Chinese were capitalists, hence anti-Communist, because of their ethnic background and their accent. But the inspectors were allowed to search them, to strip them of everything they owned till the very last minute, to the point of humiliation. My family and I became Chinese. We called on the genes of my ancestors so that we could leave with the tacit consent of the police.

My maternal great-grandfather was Chinese. He arrived in Vietnam by chance at the age of eighteen, married a Vietnamese woman and had eight children. Four of them chose to be Vietnamese, the other four Chinese. The four Vietnamese, including my grandfather, became politicians and scientists. The four Chinese prospered in the rice business. Even though my grandfather became a prefect, he could not persuade his four Chinese siblings to send their children to a Vietnamese school. And the Vietnamese clan didn't speak a word of Szechuanese. The family was divided in two, as was the country: in the South, pro-American, in the North, Communist.

My uncle Chung, my mother's big brother, was the bridge between the two political camps. In fact, his name means *together*, but I call him Uncle Two because it is a South Vietnamese tradition to replace the names of brothers and sisters with their birth order, beginning with the number two.

Uncle Two, the eldest son in the family, was a member of parliament and leader of the opposition. He belonged to a political party made up of young intellectuals who situated themselves in a third camp, daring to stand between the two lines of fire. The pro-American government had permitted the birth of that party to appease the anger and turmoil of the young idealists. My uncle had achieved top billing in the mind of the public. On one hand, his political program appealed to the members of his team. On the other, thanks to his movie-star good looks, to his constituents he represented the hope for a semblance of democracy. A charismatic, happy-go-lucky young man, he had taken down the frontier between the Chinese and Vietnamese families. He was someone who could discuss with a cabinet minister the impact of a paper shortage on freedom of the press while at the same time wrapping his arm around the waist of the man's wife and leading her in a waltz—even though the Vietnamese didn't waltz.

All through my childhood, I had a secret wish: to be Uncle Two's daughter. Sao Mai was his princess, even if he sometimes forgot her existence for days at a time. Sao Mai was revered by her parents like a prima donna. Uncle Two had many parties at their house. And often, in the middle of the evening, he would stop all conversation to seat his daughter on the piano bench and introduce the little melody she was going to play. For him, during the two short minutes of "Au clair de la lune," nothing existed but the chubby-fingered doll tinkling away with the greatest of ease before an audience of adults. Every time, I sat under the staircase to memorize my uncle's kiss on Sao Mai's nose while his guests applauded. He gave her only two minutes of attention now and then, but it was enough to give my cousin an inner strength that I lacked. It didn't matter if her stomach was empty or full, Sao Mai never hesitated to boss around her big brothers and me.

My cousin Sao Mai and I were brought up together. Either I was at her house or she was at mine. Sometimes at her place there wasn't even a grain of rice. When her parents were away, the maids disappeared too—often with the jar of rice. And her parents were often away. One day her big brother fed us some stale rice stuck to the bottom of a pan. He'd added a little oil and some green onion to make it into a meal. Five of us nibbled on that dried-up cake of rice. Other days we were buried under mountains of mangoes, longans, lychees, Lyon sausage, cream puffs.

My cousin's parents would base their choice of what to buy on the colour of a fruit or the perfume of a spice or simply according to the whim of the moment. The food they brought home was always surrounded by a festive aura, a sense of decadence and thrill. They didn't fret over the empty rice jar in the kitchen or the poems we were supposed to learn by heart. They just wanted us to stuff ourselves on mangoes, to bite into fruit and make the juice spurt, while spinning around and around like tops to the music of the Doors, Sylvie Vartan, Michel Sardou, the Beatles or Cat Stevens.

At my house, meals were always on time, the maids in attendance, homework supervised. Unlike Sao Mai's parents, my mother gave us only two mangoes to be shared by my two brothers and me, despite the dozens more that stayed in the basket. If we didn't agree about the portions, she took them back and deprived us of them until we'd reached a compromise to divide up the two mangoes among the three of us. Which is why I sometimes preferred to eat dry rice with my cousins.

I wanted to be very different from my mother,
until the day I decided to have my two sons share
a bedroom, even though there were empty rooms
in the house. I wanted them to learn to stand by
one another the way my brothers and I had done.
Someone told me that bonds are forged with laughter
but even more with sharing and the frustrations of
sharing. It may be that the tears of one led to the tears
of the other in the middle of the night, because my
autistic son finally became aware of the presence of
Pascal, a big brother he'd ignored during his first
three or four years. Today, he takes palpable pleasure
from curling up in Pascal's arms, hiding behind him
in front of strangers. It may be that thanks to all that
interrupted sleep, Pascal willingly puts on his left
shoe before the right to accommodate his brother's
obsessive rigidity. So that his brother can begin his
day without irritation, without undue disruption.

My mother was probably right, then, not only to force me to share with my brothers but also to make us share with our cousins. I shared my mother with my cousin Sao Mai because she'd taken responsibility for her niece's education. We went to the same school, like twins, sitting on the same bench in the same class. Sometimes my cousin would replace our teacher when she was away, standing on her desk and brandishing a big ruler. She was five or six years old like the rest of us, but not in the least intimidated by the ruler since, unlike us, she had always been placed on a pedestal. I, on the other hand, would wet my pants because I didn't dare put my hand up, because I didn't dare walk to the door with all eyes focused on me. My cousin struck down anyone who copied my answers. She glared at anyone who made fun of my tears. She protected me because I was her shadow.

She dragged her shadow with her everywhere, but sometimes she made me run behind her like a dog, just for laughs.

When I was with Sao Mai—and I was always with Sao Mai—the waiters in what used to be the Cercle sportif de Saigon never offered me a lime soda after my tennis lessons because they'd already brought one to Sao Mai. Inside the big fences of this fashionable club were two very distinct categories of people: the elite and the servants, the infant kings in their immaculate white clothes and the barefoot youngsters who picked up the balls. I belonged to neither. I was just Sao Mai's shadow. I positioned myself behind her to eavesdrop on her father's conversations with his tennis partners at tea time. He talked about Proust while he ate madeleines, settled in his rattan armchair on the terrace of the Cercle sportif. We travelled with him through his memories of being a foreign student in Paris. He was as enthusiastic in his descriptions of the chairs in the Jardin du Luxembourg as he was about the cancan dancers' legs that went on forever. I listened to him from behind his chair, holding my breath, like a shadow, so that he wouldn't stop.

My mother often got mad at me for being too self-effacing. She told me I had to step out of the shadows, work on my outstanding features so that the light could be reflected there. Every time she tried to take me out of the shadows, out of my shadow, I drowned myself in tears to the point of exhaustion, until she left me behind on the back seat of the car, asleep in the scorching heat of Saigon. I spent more time in people's driveways than in their sitting rooms. Sometimes I woke up to the sound of children innocently whirling around the car, sticking out their tongues and snickering. My mother thought that defending myself would strengthen my muscles. In time she was able to turn me into a woman, but never into a princess.

Today, my mother regrets not bringing me up
to be a princess, because she's not my queen in
the way that Uncle Two was a king to his children.
He maintained the royal status until his death, even
though he never signed a note for the teacher,
read a report card or washed his children's dirty
hands. Sometimes my cousin and I were lucky
enough to travel on my uncle's Vespa, my cousin
standing in front, me sitting behind. Sao Mai and
I waited for him many times under the tamarind
tree in front of our primary school, until the janitor
padlocked the doors behind us. Even the men who
sold pickled mangoes, guavas with spicy salt and
chilled jicama had already left the sidewalk in front
of the school when Mai and I, dazzled by the setting
sun, would see him coming in the distance, hair
windblown, wearing a fiery smile, incomparable.

He would take us in his arms and all at once not
only were we transformed into princesses, but we
were in his eyes also the prettiest, the most highly
prized. That moment of euphoria only lasted the
length of the journey: very soon he would have a
woman in his arms, rarely the same one, who became
in turn his princess of the moment. We would wait
for him in the sitting room until the new princess
stopped being a princess. Each of those women had
the satisfaction of thinking she was the chosen one,
even if she was well aware that she was only one
among many.

My parents were very critical of Uncle Two's
casual attitude. That was why, without
Uncle Two ever asking me, I never talked about
the long waits outside school or the evenings in the
sitting rooms of unknown women. If I'd exposed
him, he wouldn't have been allowed to pick us up.
I would have lost the chance of being a princess,
of seeing my kiss transformed into a flower on his
cheek. Thirty years later, my mother would like
me to place upon her cheeks those same kisses turned
into flowers. Maybe I did become a princess in her
eyes. But I'm just her daughter, only her daughter.

From Quebec, my mother sent money to
Uncle Two's sons so they could get away by
boat as we had done. After the first wave of boat
people in the late 1970s, it no longer made sense
to send girls to sea because encounters with pirates
had become inevitable, a ritual of the journey,
an inescapable injury. So only the two older boys
set out on the fugitives' bus. They were arrested
during the journey. Their father, my uncle, my king,
had denounced them . . . Was it from fear they'd
be lost at sea or from fear of reprisals against him,
their father? When I think back on it, I remind
myself that he couldn't tell them he'd never been
their father, only their king. He must have feared
being pointed to publicly as an anti-Communist.
He was certainly afraid of appearing in public,
where he'd have been at home a short time before.
If I'd had a voice then, I'd have told him not to
denounce them. I'd have told him that I never
informed on him for being late or made mention
of his escapades.

J eanne, our good fairy with a T-shirt and pink
tights and a flower in her hair, liberated my
voice without using words. She spoke to us—her nine
Vietnamese students at the Sainte-Famille elementary
school—with music, with her fingers, her shoulders.
She showed us how to occupy the space around us by
freeing our arms, by raising our chins, by breathing
deeply. She fluttered around us like a fairy, her eyes
stroking us one by one. Her neck stretched out to
form a continuous line with her shoulder, her arm,
all the way to her fingertips. Her legs made great
circular movements as if to sweep the walls, to stir
the air. It was thanks to Jeanne that I learned how
to free my voice from the folds of my body so it could
reach my lips.

I used my voice to read to Uncle Two just before he died, in the very heart of Saigon, some of the erotic passages from Houellebecq's *Particules élémentaires*. I no longer wanted to be his princess, I'd become his angel, reminding him how he had dipped my fingers into the whipped cream on café viennois while singing *Besame, besame mucho . . .*

His body, even once it was cold, even once it was rigid, was surrounded not only by his children, by his wives—the old one and the new—by his brothers and sisters, but also by people who didn't know him. They came in the thousands to mourn his death. Some were losing their lover, some their sports reporter, others their former member of parliament, their writer, their painter, their hand at poker.

Among all these people was a gentleman who was obviously destitute. He wore a shirt with a yellowed collar and wrinkled black pants held up by an old belt. He stood in the distance, in the shade of a royal poinciana laden with flame-red blossoms, next to a mud-stained Chinese bicycle. He had waited for hours to follow the funeral procession to the graveyard, which was in the outskirts of the city, enclosed within a Buddhist temple. There again he stood off to one side, silent and unmoving. One of my aunts went over and asked him why he'd pedalled all that distance. Did he know my uncle? He replied that he didn't know him but that it was thanks to my uncle's words that he was alive, that he got up every

morning. He had lost his idol. I hadn't. I'd lost neither
my idol nor my king, only a friend who told me
his stories about women, about politics, painting,
books; and mostly about frivolity, because he hadn't
grown old before he died. He had stopped time by
continuing to enjoy himself, to live until the end
with the lightness of a young man.

So perhaps my mother doesn't need to be my queen; simply being my mother is already a lot, even if the rare kisses I place on her cheeks aren't so majestic.

My mother envied my uncle's irresponsibility, or rather his capacity for it. In spite of herself, she was also jealous of her little brother and sisters' status as king and queens. Like their older brother, her sisters are idolized by their children for a variety of reasons, one because she's the most beautiful, another the most talented, yet another the smartest . . . In my cousins' eyes, their mother is always the best. For all of us, including my aunts and cousins, my mother was only frightening. When she was a young woman, she'd represented the highest authority figure. Zealously she imposed her role of older sister on her little sisters, because she wanted to break away from her big brother, who gobbled up every presence around him.

So my mother had taken on the duties of man of the house, Minister of Education, Mother Superior, chief executive of the clan. She made decisions, handed out punishments, put right delinquents, silenced protesters . . . My grandfather, as chairman of the board, didn't look after everyday tasks. My grandmother had her hands full raising her young children and recovering from repeated miscarriages. According to my mother, Uncle Two was the embodiment of selfishness and egocentricity. And so she became established as manager of the supreme authority. I remember one day when my grandmother didn't even dare ask her to unlock the bathroom door and release her little brother and

sisters who were being punished for going out
with Uncle Two without my mother's permission.
As she was only a young girl, she administered her
authority—naively—with an iron hand. Her revenge
against her older brother's nonchalance and the
way the children revered him was poorly planned,
because the youngsters went on playing in the
bathroom, and did it without her. All the fun of
childhood slipped between her fingers while, in
the name of propriety, she was forbidding her
sisters to dance.

Over the past ten years, however, my mother has discovered the joys of dancing. She let her friends persuade her that the tango, the cha-cha and the paso doble could replace physical exercise, that there was nothing sensual or seductive or intoxicating about them. Yet ever since she's been going to her weekly dancing class, she says now and then that she wishes she'd segued from her days on the election campaign to the parties where her brother, my father and dozens of other young candidates amused themselves around a table. Also, today she seeks my father's hand at a movie and his kiss on her cheek when posing for photos.

My mother started to live, to let herself be carried away, to reinvent herself at the age of fifty-five.

As for my father, he didn't have to reinvent himself. He is someone who lives in the moment, with no affection for the past. He savours every instant of the present as if it were still the best and only time, with no comparisons, no measurements. That's why he always inspired the greatest, most wonderful happiness, whether holding a mop on the steps of a hotel or sitting in a limousine en route to a strategic meeting with his minister.

From my father I inherited the permanent feeling of satisfaction. Where did he find it, though? Was it because he was the tenth child? Or because of the long wait for his kidnapped father's release? Before the French left Vietnam, before the Americans arrived, the Vietnamese countryside was terrorized by different factions of thugs introduced there by the French authorities to divide the country. It was common practice to sell wealthy families a nail to pay the ransom of someone who'd been kidnapped. If the nail wasn't bought, it was hammered into an earlobe—or elsewhere—on the kidnap victim. My grandfather's nail was bought by his family. When he came home, he sent his children to urban centres to live with cousins, thereby ensuring their safety and their access to education. Very early, my father learned how to live far away from his parents, to leave places, to love the present tense, to let go of any attachment to the past.

That is why he's never been curious to know
his real date of birth. The official date recorded
on his birth certificate at the city hall corresponds
to a day with no bombardment, no exploding mines,
no hostages taken. Parents may have thought that
their children's existence began on the first day that
life went back to normal, not at the moment of their
first breath.

Similarly, he has never felt the need to see Vietnam
again after his departure. Today, people from his
birthplace visit him on behalf of property developers,
suggesting he demand the deed to his father's house.
They say that ten families live there now. The last
time we saw it, it was being used as a barracks by
Communist soldiers recycled as firemen. Those
soldiers started their families in the big house.
Do they know that they live in a building put up
by a French engineer, a graduate of the prestigious
National School of Bridges and Roads? Do they
know that the house is a thank-you from my
great-uncle to my grandfather, his older brother,
who sent him to France for his education? Do they
know that ten children were brought up there but
now live in ten different cities because they were
ejected from their family circle? No, they know
nothing. They can't know: they were born after the
French withdrawal and before that part of the history
of Vietnam could be taught to them. They'd probably
never seen an American face up close, without

camouflage, until the first tourists came to their town some years ago. They only know that if my father takes back the house and sells it to a developer, they will receive a small fortune, a reward for confining my paternal grandparents to the tiniest room in their own house during the final months of their lives.

Some nights the firefighter-soldiers, drunk and lost, would fire through the curtains to silence my grandfather. But he'd stopped speaking after his stroke, which had happened before I was even born. I never heard his voice.

My paternal grandfather I never saw in any position but horizontal, stretched out on an enormous ebony daybed that stood on carved feet. He was always dressed in immaculately white pyjamas without a crease. My father's Sister Five, who had turned her back on marriage to look after her parents, kept watch obsessively over my grandfather's cleanliness. She would not tolerate the slightest spot or any sign of inattention. At mealtimes, a servant would sit behind him to keep his back straight, while my aunt fed him rice, a mouthful at a time. His favourite meal was rice with roast pork. The slices of pork were cut so finely they seemed to be minced. But they weren't to be chopped, only cut into small pieces two millimetres square. She mixed them with steaming rice served in a blue and white bowl with a silver ring around its rim to prevent chipping. If the bowls were held up to the sun, one could see translucent areas in the embossed parts. Their quality was confirmed by the glimmers that exposed the shades of blue in the patterns. The bowls nestled gently in my aunt's hands at every meal, every day, for many years. She would hold one, delicate and warm, in her fingers and add a few drops of soy sauce and a small piece of Bretel butter that was imported from France in a red tin with gold lettering. I was also entitled to this rice now and then when we visited.

Today, my father prepares this dish for my sons
when he's given some Bretel butter by friends coming
home from France. My brothers make affectionate
fun of my father because he uses the most outrageous
superlatives to describe the tinned butter. I agree with
him, though. I love the scent of that butter because it
reminds me of my paternal grandfather, the one who
died with the soldier-firemen.

I also like to use those blue bowls with the silver
rims to serve ice cream to my sons. They are the only
objects that I wanted from my aunt, the one who was
driven out of her house after the death of my paternal
grandparents. She became a Buddhist, living in a hut
behind a plantation of palm trees, stripped of all
material goods but a wooden bed without a mattress,
a sandalwood fan and her father's four blue bowls.
She hesitated briefly before complying with my
request: the bowls symbolized her last attachment
to any earthly concerns. She died shortly after
my visit to her hut, surrounded by monks from
a nearby temple.

I went back to Vietnam to work for three years,
but I never visited my father's birthplace some
two hundred and fifty kilometres from Saigon.
When I was a child, I would vomit the whole
way whenever I made that twelve-hour journey,
even though my mother put pillows on the floor of
the car to keep me still. The roads were riddled with
deep fissures. Communist rebels planted mines by
night and pro-American soldiers cleared them away
by day. Still, sometimes a mine exploded. Then we
had to wait hours for the soldiers to fill in the holes
and gather up the human remains. One day a woman
was torn to pieces, surrounded by yellow squash
blossoms, scattered, fragmented. She must have
been on her way to the market to sell her vegetables.
Maybe they also found the body of her baby by the
roadside. Or not. Maybe her husband had died in
the jungle. Maybe she was the woman who had
lost her lover outside the house of my maternal
grandfather, the prefect.

One day when we were deep inside the darkness of a cube van on our way to pick strawberries or beans, my mother told me about a woman, a day labourer, who would wait for her employer across from my maternal grandfather's place every morning. And every morning my grandfather's gardener brought her a portion of sticky rice wrapped in a banana leaf. Every morning, standing in the truck that was taking her to the rubber trees, she watched the gardener move away in the middle of the bougainvillea garden. One morning she didn't see him cross the dirt road to bring her breakfast. Then another morning . . . and another. One night she gave my mother a sheet of paper darkened with question marks, nothing else. My mother never saw her again in the truck jam-packed with workers. That young girl never went back to the plantations or to the bougainvillea garden. She disappeared not knowing that the gardener had asked his parents in vain for permission to marry her. No one told her that my grandfather had accepted the request of the gardener's parents to send him to another town. No one told her that the gardener, her own love, had been forced to go away, unable to leave her a letter because she was illiterate, because she was a young woman travelling in the company of men, because her skin had been burned too dark by the sun.

M adame Girard had the same burned skin even though she didn't work in the strawberry fields or the plantations. Madame Girard had hired my mother to clean her house, not knowing that my mother had never held a broom in her hands before her first day on the job. Madame Girard was a platinum blonde like Marilyn Monroe, with blue, blue eyes, and Monsieur Girard, a tall, brown-haired man, was the proud owner of a sparkling antique car. They often invited us to their white house with its perfectly mown lawn and flowers lining the entrance and a carpet in every room. They were the personification of our American dream.

Their daughter invited me to her roller skating competitions. She passed on to me her dresses that had become too small, one of them a blue cotton sundress with tiny white flowers and two straps that tied on the shoulder. I wore it during the summer, but also in winter over a white turtleneck. During our first winters, we didn't know that every garment had its season, that we mustn't simply wear all the clothes we owned. When we were cold, without discriminating, without knowing the different categories, we would put one garment over another, layer by layer, like the homeless.

My father tracked down Monsieur Girard thirty years later. He no longer lived in the same house, his wife had left him and his daughter was on sabbatical, in search of a purpose, a life. When my father brought me this news, I almost felt guilty. I wondered if we hadn't unintentionally stolen Monsieur Girard's American dream from having wanted it too badly.

I also got back together with my first friend, Johanne, thirty years later. She didn't recognize me, neither on the phone nor in person, because she had known me as deaf and mute. We'd never spoken. She didn't really remember that she'd wanted to become a surgeon, even though I had always told my high school guidance counsellors that I was interested in surgery, like Johanne.

The guidance counsellors would call me into their offices every year because there was a glaring gap between my grades and the results of my IQ tests, which bordered on deficient. How could I not find the intruder in the series "syringe, scalpel, skull, drill" when I could recite by heart a passage about Jacques Cartier? I only mastered what had been specifically taught to me, passed on to me, offered to me. Which is why I understood the word *surgeon* but not *darling* or *tanning salon* or *horseback riding*. I could sing the national anthem but not "The Chicken Dance" or the birthday song. I accumulated knowledge at random, like my son Henri, who can pronounce *poire* but not *maman*, because the course of our learning was atypical, full of detours and snags, with no gradation, no logic. I shaped my dreams in the same way, through meetings, friends, other people.

For many immigrants, the American dream has come true. Some thirty years ago, in Washington, Quebec City, Boston, Rimouski or Toronto, we would pass through whole neighbourhoods strewn with rose gardens, hundred-year-old trees, stone houses, but the address we were looking for never appeared on one of those doors. Nowadays, my aunt Six and her husband, Step-uncle Six, live in one of those houses. They travel first class and have to stick a sign on the back of their seat so the hostesses will stop offering them chocolates and champagne. Thirty years ago, in our Malaysian refugee camp, the same Step-uncle Six crawled more slowly than his eight-month-old daughter because he was suffering from malnutrition. And the same Aunt Six used the one needle she had to sew clothes so she could buy milk for her daughter. Thirty years ago, we lived in the dark with them, with no electricity, no running water, no privacy. Today, we complain that their house is too big and our extended family too small to experience the same intensity of the festivities—which lasted until dawn—when we used to get together at my parents' place during our first years in North America.

There were twenty-five of us, sometimes thirty, arriving in Montreal from Fanwood, Montpelier, Springfield, Guelph, coming together in a small, three-bedroom apartment for the entire Christmas holiday. Anyone who wanted to sleep alone had to move into the bathtub. Inevitably, conversations, laughter and quarrels went on all night. Every gift we offered was a genuine gift, because it represented a sacrifice and it answered a need, a desire or a dream. We were well acquainted with the dreams of our nearest and dearest: those with whom we were packed in tightly for nights at a time. Back then, we all had the same dreams. For a long time, we were obliged to have the same one, the American dream.

When I turned fifteen, my aunt Six, who at the time was working in a chicken processing plant, gave me a square aluminum tin of tea that had images of Chinese spirits, cherry trees and clouds in red, gold and black. Aunt Six had written on each of ten pieces of paper, folded in two and placed in the tea, the name of a profession, an occupation, a dream that she had for me: journalist, cabinetmaker, diplomat, lawyer, fashion designer, flight attendant, writer, humanitarian worker, director, politician. It was thanks to that gift that I learned there were other professions than medicine, that I was allowed to dream my own dreams.

Once it's achieved, though, the American dream never leaves us, like a graft or an excrescence. The first time I carried a briefcase, the first time I went to a restaurant school for young adults in Hanoi, wearing heels and a straight skirt, the waiter for my table didn't understand why I was speaking Vietnamese with him. At first I thought that he couldn't understand my southern accent. At the end of the meal, though, he explained ingenuously that I was too fat to be Vietnamese.

I translated that remark to my employers, who laugh about it to this day. I understood later that he was talking not about my forty-five kilos but about the American dream that had made me more substantial, heavier, weightier. That American dream had given confidence to my voice, determination to my actions, precision to my desires, speed to my gait and strength to my gaze. That American dream made me believe I could have everything, that I could go around in a chauffeur-driven car while estimating the weight of the squash being carried on a rusty bicycle by a woman with eyes blurred by sweat; that I could dance to the same rhythm as the girls who swayed their hips at the bar to dazzle men whose thick billfolds were swollen with American dollars; that I could live in the grand villa of an expatriate and accompany barefoot children to their school that sat right on the sidewalk, where two streets intersected.

But the young waiter reminded me that I couldn't have everything, that I no longer had the right to declare I was Vietnamese because I no longer had their fragility, their uncertainty, their fears. And he was right to remind me.

Around that time, my employer, who was based in Quebec, clipped an article from a Montreal paper reiterating that the "Québécois nation" was Caucasian, that my slanting eyes automatically placed me in a separate category, even though Quebec had given me my American dream, even though it had cradled me for thirty years. Whom to like, then? No one or everyone? I chose to like the gentleman from Saint-Félicien who asked me in English to grant him a dance. "Follow the guy," he told me. I also like the rickshaw driver in Da Nang who asked me how much I was paid as an escort for my "white" husband. And I often think about the woman who sold cakes of tofu for five cents each, sitting on the ground in a hidden corner of the market in Hanoi, who told her neighbours that I was from Japan, that I was making good progress with my Vietnamese.

She was right. I had to relearn my mother tongue, which I'd given up too soon. In any case, I hadn't really mastered it completely because the country was divided in two when I was born. I come from the South, so I had never heard people from the North until I went back to Vietnam. Similarly, people in the North had never heard people from the South before reunification. Like Canada, Vietnam had its own two solitudes. The language of North Vietnam had developed in accordance with its political, social and economic situation at the time, with words to describe

how to shoot down an airplane with a machine gun
set up on a roof, how to use monosodium glutamate
to make blood clot more quickly, how to spot the
shelters when the sirens go off. Meanwhile, the
language of the South had created words to express
the sensation of Coca-Cola bubbles on the tongue,
terms for naming spies, rebels, Communist
sympathizers on the streets of the South, names
to designate the children born from wild nights
with GIs.

It was thanks to the GIs that my step-uncle Six was able to buy his own passage and those of his wife, my aunt Six, and his very small daughter on the same boat as us. The parents of that step-uncle became very rich thanks to ice. American soldiers would buy entire blocks one metre long and twenty centimetres wide and thick to put under their beds. They needed to cool down after weeks of sweating with fear in the Vietnamese jungle. They needed human comfort, but without feeling the heat of their own bodies or of women rented by the hour. They needed the cool breezes of Vermont or Montana. They needed that coolness so they could stop suspecting, for a moment, that a grenade was hidden in the hands of every child who touched the hair on their arms. They needed that cold so as not to give way to all those full lips murmuring false words of love into their ears, to drive away the cries of their comrades with mutilated bodies. They needed to be cold to leave the women who were carrying their children without ever returning to see them again, without ever revealing their last names.

Most of those children of GIs became orphans, homeless, ostracized not only because of their mothers' profession but also because of their fathers'. They were the hidden side of the war. Thirty years after the last GI had left, the United States went back to Vietnam in place of their soldiers to rehabilitate those damaged children. The government granted them a whole new identity to erase the one that had been tarnished. A number of those children now had, for the first time, an address, a residence, a full life. Some, though, were unable to adapt to such wealth.

Once, when I was working as an interpreter for the New York police, I met one of those children, now adult. She was illiterate, wandering the streets of the Bronx. She'd come to Manhattan on a bus from a place she couldn't name. She hoped that the bus would take her back to her bed made of cardboard boxes, just outside the post office in Saigon. She declared insistently that she was Vietnamese. Even though she had café au lait skin, thick wavy hair, African blood, deep scars, she was Vietnamese, only Vietnamese, she repeated incessantly. She begged me to translate for the policeman her desire to go back to her own jungle. But the policeman could only release her into the jungle of the Bronx. Had I been able to, I would have asked her to curl up against me. Had I been able to, I'd have erased every trace of dirty hands from her body. I was the same age as her. No, I don't

have the right to say that I was the same age as her:
her age was measured in the number of stars she
saw when she was being beaten and not in years,
months, days.

At times, the memory of that girl still haunts me. I wonder what her chances of survival were in the city of New York. Or if she is still there. Whether the policeman thinks about her as often as I do. Perhaps my step-uncle Six, who has a doctorate in statistics from Princeton, could calculate the number of risks and obstacles she has faced.

I often ask that step-uncle to do the calculation, even if he has never calculated the miles travelled every morning for one whole summer to take me to my English lessons, or the quantity of books he bought me or the number of dreams he and his wife have created for me. I allow myself to ask him many things. But I've never dared to ask if it was possible for him to calculate the probability of survival for Monsieur An.

Monsieur An arrived in Granby on the same bus as our family. In winter and summer alike, Monsieur An stood with his back against the wall, and one foot on the low railing, holding a cigarette. He was our next-door neighbour. For a long time, I thought he was mute. If I ran into him today, I would say that he's autistic. One day his foot slipped on the morning dew. And bang, he was spread out on his back. BANG! He cried out "BANG!" several times, then burst out laughing. I knelt down to help him get up. He leaned against me, holding my arms, but didn't get up. He was crying. He kept crying and crying, then stopped suddenly, and turned my face towards the sky. He asked me what colour I saw. Blue. Then he raised his thumb and pointed his index finger towards my temple, asking me again if the sky was still blue.

B efore Monsieur An's job was to clean the floor of the rubber-boot plant in Granby, he'd been a judge, a professor, graduate of an American university, father and prisoner. Between the heat in his Saigon courtroom and the smell of rubber, for two years he had been accused of being a judge, of sentencing Communist countrymen. In the re-education camp, it was his turn to be judged, to position himself in the ranks every morning with hundreds of others who'd also been on the losing side in the war.

That camp surrounded by jungle was a retreat for the prisoners to assess and formulate self-criticisms, depending on their status—counter-revolutionary; traitor to the nation; collaborator with the Americans—and to meditate on their redemption while felling trees, planting corn, clearing fields of mines.

The days followed one another like the links of a chain—the first fastened around their necks, the last to the centre of the earth. One morning, Monsieur An felt his chain getting shorter when the soldiers took him out of the ranks and made him kneel in the mud before the fleeting, frightened, empty gazes of his former colleagues, their bodies barely covered with rags and skin. He told me that when the hot metal of the pistol touched his temple, in one last act of rebellion he raised his head to look at the sky. For the first time, he could see shades of blue, all equally intense. Together, they dazzled him almost to the point of blindness. At the same time, he could hear the click of the trigger drop into silence. No sound, no explosion, no blood, only sweat. That night, the shades of blue that he'd seen earlier filed past his eyes like a film being screened over and over.

He survived. The sky had cut his chain, had saved him, freed him, while some of the others were suffocated to death, dried up in containers without having a chance to count the blues of the sky. Every day, then, he set himself the task of listing those colours—for the others.

Monsieur An taught me about nuance.
Monsieur Minh gave me the urge to write.
I met Monsieur Minh on a red vinyl bench in a
Chinese restaurant on Côte-des-Neiges where my
father worked as a delivery man. I did my homework
while I waited for the end of his shift. Monsieur Minh
made notes for him about one-way streets, private
addresses, clients to avoid. He was preparing to
become a delivery man just as seriously, just as
enthusiastically, as he'd studied French literature
at the Sorbonne. He was saved not by the sky but by
writing. He had written a number of books during
his time in the re-education camp—always on the
one piece of paper he possessed, page by page,
chapter by chapter, an unending story. Without
writing, he wouldn't have heard the snow melting
or leaves growing or clouds sailing through the sky.
Nor would he have seen the dead end of a thought,
the remains of a star or the texture of a comma.
Nights when he was in his kitchen painting wooden
ducks, Canada geese, loons, mallards, following
the colour scheme provided by his other employer,
he would recite for me the words in his personal
dictionary: nummular, moan, quadraphony, *in
extremis*, sacculina, logarithmic, hemorrhage—like
a mantra, like a march towards the void.

Each of us had been saved in a different way during Vietnam's peacetime or postwar period. My own family was saved by Anh Phi.

It was Anh Phi, teenage son of a friend of my parents, who found the pack of gold taels my father had flung from our third-floor balcony during the night. The day before, my parents had told me to pull on the bit of rope that ran alongside the corridor if one of the ten soldiers living in our house should come up to our floor. My parents had spent hours in the bathroom clearing out the thin gold sheets and the diamonds hidden under the tiny pink and black tiles. Then they wrapped them carefully in several layers of brown paper bags before throwing them into the dark. The package had landed as expected in the debris of the demolished house that once belonged to the former neighbour across the way.

At that time, children had to plant trees as a sign of gratitude towards our spiritual leader, Ho Chi Minh, and they also had to retrieve undamaged bricks from demolition sites. My search through the debris for the package of gold therefore roused no suspicions. But I had to be careful, because one of the soldiers at our house was assigned to keep an eye on where we went and whom we were with. Knowing that I was being watched, I walked across the site too quickly and couldn't find the package, not even after a second try. My parents asked Anh Phi to take a look. After his search, he took off with a bag full of bricks.

The package of gold taels was returned to my parents a few days later. Subsequently, they gave it to the organizer of our sea-bound escape. All the taels were there. During this chaotic peacetime, it was the norm for hunger to replace reason, for uncertainty to usurp morality, but the reverse was rarely true. Anh Phi and his mother were the exception. They became our heroes.

To tell the truth, Anh Phi had been my hero long before he handed over the two and a half kilos of gold to my parents, because whenever I visited him, he would sit with me on his doorstep and make a candy appear from behind my ear instead of urging me to play with the other children.

My first journey on my own, without my parents, was to Texas, to see Anh Phi again and this time give him a candy. We were sitting side by side on the floor against his single bed in the university residence when I asked him why he'd given the package of gold back to my parents, when his widowed mother had to mix their rice with barley, sorghum and corn to feed him and his three brothers. Why that heroically honest deed? He told me, laughing and hitting me repeatedly with his pillow, that he wanted my parents to be able to pay for our passage because otherwise he wouldn't have a little girl to tease. He was still a hero, a true hero, because he couldn't help being one, because he is a hero without knowing it, without wanting to be.

I wanted to be a heroine to the young girl selling grilled pork outside the walls of the Buddhist temple across from the office in Hanoi. She spoke very little, was always working, absorbed in the slices of pork she was cutting then putting into the dozens of baguettes she'd already split down three-quarters of their length. It was hard to see her face once the coal had been kindled in the metal box blackened by grease accumulated over the years, because a cloud of smoke and ash enveloped her, suffocated her, made her eyes water. Her brother-in-law served the customers and washed the dishes in two pots of water set on the very edge of the sidewalk, beside an open sewer. She must have been fifteen or sixteen, and was stunningly beautiful despite her misty eyes and her cheeks smeared with ashes and soot.

One day her hair caught fire, burning part of her polyester shirt before her brother-in-law had time to pour the dirty dishwater over her head. She was covered with lettuce, slices of green papaya, hot peppers, fish sauce. I went to see her before lunch the next day to offer her work cleaning the office and to suggest that she sign up for a cooking class and English lessons. I was sure I would be granting her fondest dream. But she refused, refused all of it, by simply shaking her head. I left Hanoi, abandoning her to her bit of sidewalk, unable to make her turn

her gaze towards a horizon without smoke, unable
to become a hero like Anh Phi, like many people
who have been identified, named and designated
heroes in Vietnam.

Peace born from the mouths of cannon inevitably gives birth to hundreds, to thousands of anecdotes about the brave, about heroes. During the first years after the Communist victory, there weren't enough pages in the history books to fit in all the heroes, so they were lodged in math books: if Comrade Công downed two airplanes a day, how many did he shoot down in a week?

We no longer learned to count with bananas and pineapples. The classroom was turned into a huge game of Risk, with calculations of dead, wounded or imprisoned soldiers and patriotic victories, grandiose and colourful. The colours, though, were illustrated only with words. Pictures were monochromatic, like the people, perhaps to stop us from forgetting the dark side of reality. We all had to wear black pants and dark shirts. If not, soldiers in khaki uniforms would take us to the station for a session of interrogation and re-education. They also arrested girls who used blue eyeshadow. They thought these girls had black eyes, that they were victims of capitalist violence. Perhaps for that reason they removed the sky blue from the first Vietnamese Communist flag.

When my husband wore his red T-shirt with a yellow star in the streets of Montreal, the Vietnamese harassed him. Later my parents had him take it off and replaced it with an ill-fitting shirt of my father's. Even though I could never have worn such a thing myself, I hadn't told my husband not to buy it because I myself had once proudly tied a red scarf around my neck. I had made that symbol of Communist youth part of my wardrobe. I even envied friends who had the words *Cháu ngoan Bác Hồ* embroidered in yellow on the triangle that jutted out from the neckline. They were the "beloved children of the party," a status I could never attain because of my family background, even though I stood first in my class or had planted the most trees while thinking about the father of our peace. Every classroom, every office, every house was supposed to have at least one photo of Ho Chi Minh on the walls. His photo even displaced those of ancestors that no one had ever dared to touch before because they were sacred. The ancestors—though they may have been gamblers, incompetent or violent—all became respectable and untouchable once they were dead, once they'd been placed on the altar with incense, fruits, tea. The altars had to be high enough so that the ancestors looked down on us. All descendants had to carry their ancestors not in their hearts but above their heads.

J ust recently in Montreal, I saw a Vietnamese grandmother ask her one-year-old grandson: *"Thương Bà để đâu?"* I can't translate that phrase, which contains just four words, two of them verbs, *to love* and *to carry*. Literally, it means, "Love grandmother carry where?" The child touched his head with his hand. I had completely forgotten that gesture, which I'd performed a thousand times when I was small. I'd forgotten that love comes from the head and not the heart. Of the entire body, only the head matters. Merely touching the head of a Vietnamese person insults not just him but his entire family tree. That is why a shy Vietnamese eight-year-old turned into a raging tiger when his Québécois teammate rubbed the top of his head to congratulate him for catching his first football.

If a mark of affection can sometimes be taken for an insult, perhaps the gesture of love is not universal: it too must be translated from one language to another, must be learned. In the case of Vietnamese, it is possible to classify, to quantify the meaning of love through specific words: to love by taste (*thích*); to love without being in love (*thương*); to love passionately (*yêu*); to love ecstatically (*mê*); to love blindly (*mù quáng*); to love gratefully (*tình nghĩa*). It's impossible quite simply to love, to love without one's head.

I am lucky that I've learned to savour the pleasure of resting my head in a hand, and my parents are

lucky to be able to capture the love of my children
when the little ones drop kisses into their hair,
spontaneously, with no formality, during a session
of tickling in bed. I myself have touched my father's
head only once. He had ordered me to lean on it as
I stepped over the handrail of the boat.

We didn't know where we were. We had landed on the first terra firma. As we were making our way to the beach, an Asian man in light blue boxer shorts came running towards our boat. He told us in Vietnamese to disembark and destroy the boat. Was he Vietnamese? Were we back at our starting point after four days at sea? I don't think anyone asked, because we all jumped into the water as if we were an army being deployed. The man disappeared into this chaos, for good. I don't know why I've held on to such a clear image of that man running in the water, arms waving, fist punching the air with an urgent cry that the wind didn't carry to me. I remember that image with as much precision and clarity as the one of Bo Derek running out of the water in her flesh-coloured bathing suit. Yet I saw that man only once, for a fraction of a second, unlike the poster of Bo Derek, which I would come upon every day for months.

Everyone on deck saw him. But no one dared confirm it with certainty. He may have been one of the dead who had seen the local authorities drive the boats back to the sea. Or a ghost whose duty it was to save us, so he could gain his own access to paradise. He may have been a schizophrenic Malaysian. Or maybe a tourist from a Club Med who wanted to break the monotony of his vacation.

M ost likely he was a tourist, because we landed on a beach that was protected because of its turtle population, and it was close to the site of a Club Med. In fact, this beach had once been part of a Club Med, because their beachside bar still existed. We slept there every day against the backdrop of the bar's wall, which was inscribed with the names of Vietnamese people who'd stopped by, who had survived like us. If we'd waited fifteen minutes longer before berthing, our feet wouldn't have been wedged in the fine golden sand of this heavenly beach. Our boat was completely destroyed by the waves created by an ordinary rain that fell immediately after we disembarked. More than two hundred of us watched in silence, eyes misty from rain and astonishment. The wooden planks skipped one at a time on the crest of the waves, like a synchronized swimming routine. I'm positive that for one brief moment the sight made believers of us all. Except one man. He'd retraced his steps to fetch the gold taels he'd hidden in the boat's fuel tank. He never came back. Perhaps the taels made him sink, perhaps they were too heavy to carry. Or else the current swallowed him as punishment for looking back, or to remind us that we must never regret what we've left behind.

That memory definitely explains why I never leave a place with more than one suitcase. I take only books. Nothing else can become truly mine. I sleep just as well in a hotel room, a guest room or a stranger's bed as in my own. In fact, I'm always glad to move; it gives me a chance to lighten my belongings, to leave objects behind so that my memory can become truly selective, can remember only images that stay luminous behind my closed eyelids. I prefer to remember the flutters in my stomach, my light-headedness, my upheavals, my hesitations, my lapses . . . I prefer them because I can shape them according to the colour of time, whereas an object remains inflexible, frozen, unwieldy.

I love men in the same way, without wanting them to be mine. That way, I am one among others, without a role to play, without existing. I don't need their presence because I don't miss those who are absent. They're always replaced or replaceable. If they're not, my feelings for them are. For that reason, I prefer married men, their hands dressed in gold rings. I like those hands on my body, on my breasts. I like them because, despite the mixture of odours, despite the dampness of their skin on mine, despite the occasional euphoria, those ring fingers with their histories keep me remote, aloof, in the shadows.

I forget the details of how I felt during these encounters. I do remember fleeting gestures, such as Guillaume's finger brushing against my left baby toe to write his initial G; the drop of sweat from Mikhaïl's chin falling onto my first lumbar vertebra; the cavity at the bottom of Simon's breastbone, Simon who told me that if I murmured into the well of his *pectus excavatum*, my words would resonate all the way to his heart.

Over the years, I've collected a fluttering eyelash from one, a stray lock of hair from another, lessons from some, silences from several, an afternoon here, an idea there—to form just one lover, because I've neglected to memorize the face of each one. Together, these men taught me how to become a lover, how to be in love, how to long for an amorous state. It's my children, though, who have taught me the verb *to love*, who have defined it. If I had known what it meant to love, I wouldn't have had children, because once we love, we love forever, like Uncle Two's wife, Step-aunt Two, who can't stop loving her gambler son, the son who is burning up the family fortune like a pyromaniac.

When I was younger, I saw Step-aunt Two
prostrate herself before Buddha, before
Jesus, before her son, to plead with him not to go
away for months at a time, not to come back from
those months of absence escorted by men holding
a knife to his throat. Before I became a mother,
I couldn't understand how she, a businesswoman
with clenched fists, keen eyes, a sharp tongue,
could believe all the lying tales and promises of
her gambler son. During my recent visit to Saigon,
she told me she must have been a serious criminal
in her former life, if she was obliged, in this life,
to constantly believe the deceptions of her son.
She wanted to stop loving. She was tired of loving.

Because I had become a mother, I lied to her too by
remaining silent about the night her son took my
child's hand and wrapped it around his adolescent
penis, and about the night when he slipped inside
the mosquito net of Aunt Seven, the one who is
mentally retarded, defenceless. I shut my mouth
to keep my aging, worn-out step-aunt Two from
dying because she had loved so much.

Aunt Seven is my maternal grandmother's sixth child. Her number, seven, didn't bring the good luck it was supposed to. When I was a child, Aunt Seven sometimes waited for me at the door holding a wooden spatula, ready to hit me as hard as she could to drive out the heat that was stored in her body. She was always hot. She needed to cry out, to fling herself onto the floor, to let off steam by hitting. As soon as she started howling, all the servants ran through the house, leaving their bucket of water, their knife, their kettle, their dust cloth, their broom along the way, and came to hold her down. To this tumult were added the cries of my grandmother, my mother, my other aunts, their children and my own. We were a twenty-voice choir nearly hysterical, nearly mad. After a while we no longer knew why we were howling, because the original cry, Aunt Seven's, had been muffled by our own noise for so long. But everyone went on crying, taking advantage of the opportunity to do so.

Sometimes, instead of waiting for me at the door, Aunt Seven would open it after stealing the keys from my grandmother. She would open it so she could leave us and end up at large in the alleyways, where her handicap wasn't visible, or was at least ignored. Some ignored her handicap by accepting her twenty-four-carat-gold necklace in exchange for a piece of guava, or by having sex with her in exchange for a compliment. Some even hoped that

she would become pregnant so they could make the
baby the object of blackmail. At that time, my aunt
and I were the same mental age, we were friends who
told each other what scared us. We shared our stories.
Today, my handicapped aunt thinks of me as an adult,
so she doesn't tell me about her escapes or her old
stories from the alleyways.

I too dreamed of being outside, playing hopscotch
with the neighbourhood children. I envied them
through the wrought iron grilles over our windows
or from our balconies. Our house was surrounded by
cement walls two metres high with shards of broken
glass embedded in them to discourage intruders.
From where I stood, it was hard to say if the wall
existed to protect us or to remove our access to life.

The alleys were swarming with children skipping,
with ropes braided out of hundreds of multicoloured
rubber bands. My favourite toy wasn't a doll that
said, "I love you." My dream toy was a small wooden
chair with a built-in drawer where the street vendors
kept their money, and also the two big baskets they
carried at either end of a long bamboo pole balanced
on their shoulders. These women sold all kinds of
soups. They walked between the two weights: on one
side, a large cauldron of broth and a coal fire to keep
it hot; on the other, the bowls, chopsticks, rice noodles
and condiments. Sometimes the vendor might even
have a baby hanging from her back. Each merchant
advertised her wares with a particular melody.

Years later, in Hanoi a French friend of mine would
get up at five in the morning to record their songs.
He told me that before long those sounds would no
longer be heard on the streets, that those strolling
merchants would give up their baskets for factory
work. So he would safeguard their voices reverently
and ask me to translate them along the way, then he
would list them by category: merchants selling soup,
selling cream of soya, buyers of glass for recycling,
knife-grinders, masseurs for men, bread-sellers . . .
We spent whole afternoons working on translations.
With my friend, I learned that music comes from
the voice, the rhythm and the heart of each person,
and that the musicality of those unrecorded melodies
could lift the curtain of fog, pass through windows
and screens to waken us as gently as a morning lullaby.

He had to get up early to record them because
the soups were sold mainly in the morning. Each
soup had its own vermicelli: round ones with beef,
small and flat with pork and shrimp, transparent
with chicken . . . Each woman had her specialty
and her route. When Marie-France, my teacher in
Granby, asked me to describe my breakfast, I told
her: soup, vermicelli, pork. She asked me again,
more than once, miming waking up, rubbing her
eyes and stretching. But my reply was the same,
with a slight variation: rice instead of vermicelli.
The other Vietnamese children gave similar
descriptions. She called home then to check

the accuracy of our answers with our parents.
As time went on, we no longer started our day
with soup and rice. To this day, I haven't found
a substitute. So it's very rare that I have breakfast.

I went back to having soup for breakfast when I was pregnant with my son Pascal, in Vietnam. I didn't crave pickles or peanut butter, just a bowl of soup with vermicelli purchased on a street corner. Throughout my childhood, my grandmother forbade us to eat those soups because the bowls were washed in a tiny bucket of water. It was impossible for the vendors to carry water on their shoulders as well as the broth and the bowls. Whenever it was possible, they would ask people for some clean water. As a small child, I often waited for them at the fence near the kitchen door with fresh water for their buckets. I would have traded my blue-eyed doll for their wooden chairs. I should have suggested it, because today they've been replaced by plastic chairs, which are lighter, don't have a built-in drawer, and don't show the traces of fatigue and wear in their grain as wooden benches do. The merchants stepped into the modern era still carrying the weight of the yoke on their shoulders.

The trace of the red and yellow stripes of a Pom sandwich-bread bag is burned into one side of our first toaster. Our sponsors in Granby had placed that small appliance at the top of the list of essentials to buy when we moved into our first apartment. For years we lugged that toaster from one place to the next without ever using it, because our breakfast was rice, soup, leftovers from the night before. Quietly, we started eating Rice Krispies, without milk. My brothers followed this with toast and jam. Every morning for twenty years, without exception, the youngest breakfasted on two slices of sandwich bread with butter and strawberry jam, no matter where he was posted—New York, New Delhi, Moscow or Saigon. His Vietnamese maid tried to make him change his habits by offering him steaming balls of sticky rice covered with freshly grated coconut, roasted sesame seeds and peanuts crushed in a mortar, or a piece of warm baguette with ham spread with homemade mayonnaise, or pâté de foie decorated with a sprig of coriander . . . He brushed them all aside and went back to his sandwich bread, which he kept in the freezer. During my latest visit to him I discovered that he keeps our old stained toaster in a cupboard. It's the only trinket he has carted with him from country to country as if it were an anchor, or the memory of dropping the first anchor.

I discovered my own anchor when I went to meet Guillaume at Hanoi airport. The scent of Bounce fabric softener on his T-shirt made me cry. For two weeks I slept with a piece of Guillaume's clothing on my pillow. Guillaume, for his part, was dazzled by the scent of jackfruit, kumquats, durians, carambola, of bitter melons, field crabs, dried shrimp, of lilies, lotus and herbs. Several times he went to the night market where vegetables, fruit and flowers were traded back and forth between the baskets of the vendors negotiating among themselves in a noisy but controlled chaos, as if they were on the floor of the Stock Exchange. I would go to this night market with Guillaume, always with one of his pullovers over my shirt because I'd discovered that my home could be summed up as an ordinary, simple odour from my daily North American life. I had no street address of my own, I lived in an office apartment in Hanoi. My books were stored at Aunt Eight's place, my diplomas at my parents' in Montreal, my photos at my brothers', my winter coats with my former roommate. I realized for the first time that Bounce, the smell of Bounce, had given me my first attack of homesickness.

During my early years in Quebec, my clothes smelled of damp or of food because after they were washed they were hung up in our bedrooms on lines strung from wall to wall. At night, every night, my last image was of colours suspended across the room like Tibetan prayer flags. For years I inhaled the scent of fabric softener on my classmates' clothes when the wind carried it to me. I happily breathed in the bags of used clothes we received. It was the only smell I wanted.

Guillaume left Hanoi after staying with me for two weeks. He had no clean clothes to leave me. Over the following months, I received in the mail now and then a tightly sealed plastic envelope with a freshly dried handkerchief inside, smelling of Bounce. The last package he sent me contained a plane ticket for Paris. When I arrived, he was waiting to take me to an appointment with a perfumer. He wanted me to smell a violet leaf, an iris, blue cypress, vanilla, lovage . . . and, most of all, everlasting, an aroma of which Napoleon said smelled of his country before he even set foot on it. Guillaume wanted me to find an aroma that would give me my country, my world.

I've never worn any other perfume than the one that was created for me at Guillaume's request during that trip to Paris. It replaced Bounce. It speaks for me and reminds me that I exist. One of my roommates spent several years studying theology and archaeology in order to understand who our creator is, who we are, why we exist. Every night, she came back to the apartment not with answers but with new questions. I never had any questions except the one about the moment when I could die. I should have chosen the moment before the arrival of my children, for since then I've lost the option of dying. The sharp smell of their sun-baked hair, the smell of sweat on their backs when they wake from a nightmare, the dusty smell of their hands when they leave a classroom, meant that I have to live, to be dazzled by the shadow of their eyelashes, moved by a snowflake, bowled over by a tear on their cheek. My children have given me the exclusive power to blow on a wound to make the pain disappear, to understand words unpronounced, to possess the universal truth, to be a fairy. A fairy smitten with the way they smell.

Wyatt was smitten with the *ao dài* because
that outfit makes women's bodies look
gorgeously delicate and tremendously romantic.
One day he took me to a grand villa hidden behind
rows of kiosks built on the ground where the garden
had once stood. The villa was home to two aging
sisters who were quietly selling off their furniture
to collectors to ensure their day-to-day survival.
Wyatt was their most faithful customer, so we were
invited to recline on a big mahogany daybed like the
one my paternal grandfather had, resting our heads
on the ceramic cushions where opium smokers once
lay. The owner brought us tea and slices of candied
ginger. A slight breeze lifted the tails of her *ao dài*
when she bent over to set the cups between Wyatt
and me. Although she was sixty years old, the
sensuality of her *ao dài* touched us. The one square
centimetre of skin that was revealed mocked the
ravages of time: it still made our hearts leap.
Wyatt said that the diminutive space was his golden
triangle, his isle of happiness, his own private
Vietnam. Between sips of tea he whispered:
"It stirs my soul."

When soldiers from the North arrived in Saigon, they too were stirred by that triangle of skin. They were troubled by the schoolgirls in white *ao dàis*, bursting out of their school like butterflies in spring. And so wearing the *ao dài* was soon forbidden. It was banned because it cast aspersions on the heroism of the women in green kepis who appeared on enormous billboards at every street corner, in khaki shirts with sleeves rolled up on their muscular arms. They were right to banish the outfit. It took three times as long to button it than to take it off. One brisk movement was enough to make the snap fasteners pop open. My grandmother took not three but ten times longer to put on the tunic, because after giving birth to ten children her body had to be sculpted, redrawn with a girdle that had thirty hooks and eyes, to respect the cut of that hypocritically modest and deceptively candid garment.

Today, my grandmother is a very old woman,
but still beautiful, lavishly so, like a queen.
When she was in her forties, sitting in her parlour
in Saigon, she epitomized a whole era of an extreme
kind of beauty, of opulence. Every morning a cohort
of merchants waited at the door to present their finds
to her. Most of them already knew her requirements.
They brought new crockery, plastic flowers just
arrived from Europe and, inevitably, brassieres
for her six daughters. As the country was at war,
and the market unstable, it was best to anticipate
everything. Sometimes it was diamonds. All the
Vietnamese women in our circle had a loupe for
examining diamonds. I had learned very young
to spot inclusions in diamonds, because it was a skill
necessary for dealing with family finances. As the
banking system was weak and transitory, women
had to master the art of buying and selling gold and
diamonds to manage their savings. My grandmother
spent days at a time running errands without ever
moving. In the midst of the sellers' visits, she also
entertained friends or interviewed servants looking
for work.

My grandmother's days were filled with these
mundane tasks. And while she was a believer,
she didn't have time to sit in front of Buddha.
After the markets had been cleaned out of
merchandise and merchants, after her Communist
tenants had taken the contents of her safe and her

lace scarves, she learned to dress in the long grey kimono worn by the faithful. Despite her salt-and-pepper hair, which she quite simply smoothed and tied into a bun just above the nape of her neck, she was still stunningly beautiful. She said her prayers at all hours of the day, in the smoke of incense sticks, waiting for word from her children who'd gone to sea. She'd let her two youngest, a boy and a girl, leave with my mother despite the uncertainty. My mother asked my grandmother to choose between the risk of losing her son at sea and that of finding him torn to shreds in a minefield during his military service in Cambodia. She had to choose secretly, without hesitating, without trembling, without perspiring. Perhaps it was to control her fear that she started to pray. Perhaps it was to become intoxicated with the incense smoke that she no longer left the altar.

In Hanoi, I had a neighbour across the street who also prayed every morning, at dawn, for hours. Unlike my grandmother's, though, her windows made of bamboo slats opened directly onto the street. Her mantra and her steady and incessant pounding on her block of wood intruded on the whole neighbourhood. At first I wanted to move, lodge a complaint, even steal her bell and smash it to bits. After a few weeks, though, I stopped cursing the woman because I was haunted by the image of my grandmother.

During the first years of immense upsets, my grandmother sometimes took refuge in temples. She wanted so badly to hide in them that she even allowed Aunt Seven to drive her. Aunt Seven didn't know how to drive a moped, because no one had shown her, and also because she wasn't supposed to leave the house. But the rules had been rewritten since the structural upheaval of her life and of life in general. For my handicapped aunt, that bursting of the family nucleus brought a kind of freedom, as well as an opportunity to grow up. The situation led her to start up the one moped that was left in the courtyard. My grandmother got on, and my aunt began to drive and drive, never changing speed, never stopping, even at red lights. She told me later that when she saw a traffic light she closed her eyes. As for my grandmother, she put her hands on her daughter's shoulders and prayed.

I would have liked Aunt Seven to tell me about how she had given birth while with the nuns. I don't know if she's aware that Aunt Four's adopted son is actually hers. I don't know how I knew. Maybe because the children listened through keyholes without the adults noticing. Or because adults aren't always aware that children are present. The parents didn't need to keep an eye on their children; they counted on the nannies to supervise them. But parents sometimes forgot that the nannies were young girls: they too had urges, they liked to attract the eyes of the chauffeur, the smile of the tailor, they liked to dream for a moment, as they looked at themselves in the mirror, that they too were part of the backdrop reflected there.

I always had nannies, but they sometimes forgot me. And I don't remember any of them, even if I often find them in a corner, out of focus, in the photos from my childhood.

My son Pascal also lost all memory of his nanny, Lek, very soon after we left Bangkok to come home to Montreal. Yet his Thai nanny had been with him seven days a week, twenty-four hours a day, for more than two years, except for a few days' holiday now and then. Lek loved Pascal from the very first moment. She showed him off in the neighbourhood as if he were hers, the most beautiful, the most magnificent. She loved him so much I was afraid she'd forget that inevitably they would separate, that someday we were going to leave her and, sadly, my son might not remember her at all.

Lek knew just a few words of English and I a few words of Thai, but all the same we managed to have long conversations about the residents of my building. The most cinematic image was that of the ninth-floor neighbour, an American in his thirties. One night he came home from work to find his apartment covered with feathers and moss. His pants had been cut in two lengthwise, his sofas ripped open, his tables lacerated by a knife, his curtains torn to shreds. All this damage was the work of the mistress he'd dismissed after three months of service. He shouldn't have exceeded the limit of one month, because the hope of a great love grew in her mind every day, even though she continued to be paid every Friday for her loving. To avoid a disappointment on that scale, perhaps he shouldn't have invited her to all those meals where she smiled without understanding anything,

where she was a decoration for the table, where she
swallowed vichyssoise while intensely craving a salad
of green papaya with bird chilies that tore your mouth
apart, that burned your lips, set fire to your heart.

I've often asked strangers who came to Asia to
buy love on a one-time basis why, on the morning
after a wild night, they insisted on sharing their meal
with their Vietnamese or Thai mistress. The women
would have preferred to receive the cost of those
meals in cash, so they could buy a pair of shoes for
their mother or a new mattress for their father,
or to send their little brother for English lessons.
Why desire their presence outside of bed when
their vocabulary is limited to conversations that
go on behind closed doors? They told me I didn't
understand a thing. They needed those young girls
for a totally different reason—to restore their youth.
When they looked at those young girls, they saw
their own youth, filled with dreams and possibilities.
The girls gave them something: the illusion that they
hadn't made a mess of their lives, or, at the very least,
the strength and the urge to start over. Without them
they felt disillusioned, sad. Sad at having never
loved enough and having never been loved enough.
Disillusioned because money hadn't brought
them happiness, except in countries where
for five dollars they could obtain an hour of
happiness, or at least some affection, company,
attention. For five dollars they got a clumsily
made-up girl who came for a coffee or a beer
with them and roared with laughter because
the man had just said the Vietnamese word

urinate instead of *pepper*, two words differentiated only by an accent, a tone that is nearly imperceptible to the untrained ear. A single accent for a single moment of happiness.

One night, as I followed into a restaurant a man with a slashed earlobe like that of one of the Communist soldiers who'd lived in my family home in Saigon, I saw through the slit between two panels of a private room six girls lined up against the wall, teetering in their high heels, faces heavily made up, bodies frail, skin shivering, totally naked in the flickering light from the fluorescent tubes. Together, six men took aim at the girls, each with a tightly rolled American hundred-dollar bill, folded in half around a taut rubber band. The bills crossed the smoky room at the crazy speed of projectiles, finally landing on the girls' translucent skin.

During my first months in Vietnam, I was very flattered when people thought I was my boss's escort, in spite of my designer suit and my high heels, because it meant that I was still young, slim, fragile. But after witnessing the scene where the girls had to bend down to pick up the hundred-dollar bills wadded at their feet, I stopped feeling flattered out of respect for them, because behind their dreamy bodies and their youth, they carried all the invisible weight of Vietnam's history, like the women with hunched backs.

Like some of the girls whose skin was too delicate, who couldn't bear the weight, I left before the third volley. I left the restaurant deafened not by the sound of clinking glasses but by the imperceptible sound of the shock of bills against their skin. I left the restaurant, my head filled with the resonance of the stoic silence of the girls who'd stayed behind, who had the strength to strip the money of its power, becoming untouchable, invincible.

When I meet young girls in Montreal
or elsewhere who injure their bodies
intentionally, deliberately, who want permanent
scars to be drawn on their skin, I can't help secretly
wishing they could meet other young girls whose
permanent scars are so deep they're invisible to the
naked eye. I would like to seat them face to face
and hear them make comparisons between a wanted
scar and an inflicted scar, one that's paid for, the other
that pays off, one visible, the other impenetrable, one
inordinately sensitive, the other unfathomable,
one drawn, the other misshapen.

Aunt Seven also has a scar, on her lower belly, the trace of one of her escapades in the maze of alleys where she inched her way between the vendors of ice and of slippers, between squabbling neighbours, angry women and men with erections. Which of these men was the father of her child? No one dared to question Aunt Seven because they'd had to lie to her during her pregnancy to protect her from her own belly by concealing it under the habit of the nuns at the Couvent des Oiseaux. The nuns called her Josette and showed her how to write her name in large dotted characters. Josette never knew why she was getting so fat or why she woke from a deep sleep to discover that she was thin. She only knew that Aunt Four's adopted son ran away, like her, as soon as he could. He criss-crossed the same alleys at the speed of light, holding his sandals so that his feet would feel the heat of the pavement, the texture of excrement, the sharpness of a piece of broken bottle. He ran all through his childhood. And all through his childhood we other children, young and old, ten, fifteen, even twenty of us, patrolled the neighbourhood every month. One day we all came home empty-handed, as did the servants and the neighbours. He left our lives along the same trail he'd arrived on, leaving as his only souvenir a scar above his mother's pubic area.

My son Henri runs away too. He runs to the St. Lawrence River on the other side of a highway, of a boulevard, a street, a park, another street. He runs to the water where the smooth rhythm and the constant movement of the waves hypnotize him, offer him calm and protection. I've learned to be a shadow in his shadow so I can follow him without upsetting him, without harassing him. Once, though, it took just one second of distraction and I saw him dash in front of the cars, excited and full of life as never before. I was staggered by the juxtaposition of his happiness, so rare, so unexpected, and my own anguish at the thought of his body thrown up in the air above a fender. Should I close my eyes and slow down to avoid witnessing the impact, to survive? Motherhood, my own, afflicted me with a love that vandalized my heart, puffed it up, deflated it and expelled it from my rib cage when I saw my older son, Pascal, show up out of the blue, and fling his brother onto the freshly cut grass of the boulevard median. Pascal landed on his brother like an angel, with chubby little thighs, candy-pink cheeks and a tiny thumb sticking up in the air.

I cried with joy as I took my two sons by the hand, but I cried as well because of the pain of that other Vietnamese mother who witnessed her son's execution. An hour before his death, that boy was running across the rice paddy with the wind in his hair, to deliver messages from one man to another, from one hand to another, from one hiding place to another, to prepare for the revolution, to do his part for the resistance, but also, sometimes, to help send a simple love note on its way.

That son was running with his childhood in his legs. He couldn't see the very real risk of being picked up by soldiers of the enemy camp. He was six years old, maybe seven. He couldn't read yet. All he knew was how to hold tightly in his hands the scrap of paper he'd been given. Once he was captured, though, standing in the midst of rifles pointed at him, he no longer remembered where he was running to, or the name of the person the note was addressed to, or his precise starting point. Panic muted him. Soldiers silenced him. His frail body collapsed on the ground and the soldiers left, chewing their gum. His mother ran across the rice paddy where traces of her son's footprints were still fresh. In spite of the sound of the bullet that had torn space open, the landscape stayed the same. The young rice shoots continued to be cradled by the wind, imperturbable in the face of the brutality

of those oversized loves, of the pains too muted for
tears to flow, for cries to escape from that mother
who gathered up in her old mat the body of her son,
half buried in the mud.

I held back my cries so as not to distort the hypnotic
sound of the sewing machines standing one
behind the other in my parents' garage. Like my
brothers and me, my cousins sewed after school for
pocket money. With eyes focused on the regular,
rapid movement of the needles, we didn't see one
another, so that very often our conversations were
actually confessions. My cousins were only ten years
old, but they already had a past to recount because
they'd been born into an exhausted Saigon and
had grown up during Vietnam's darkest period.
They described to me, with mocking laughter,
how they had masturbated men in exchange for
a bowl of soup at two thousand dongs. Holding
nothing back, they described those sex acts naturally
and honestly, as people for whom prostitution is
merely a question of adults and money, a matter
that does not involve children six or seven years old
like them, who did it in exchange for a fifteen-cent
meal. I listened to them without turning around,
still sewing, without commenting, because I wanted
to protect the innocence in their words, not tarnish
their candour by my interpretation of the act.
It was certainly thanks to that innocence that
they became engineers after ten years of studies
in Montreal and Sherbrooke.

Coming home after leaving my cousins at the University of Sherbrooke, I was approached in a gas station by a Vietnamese man who had recognized my vaccination scar. One look at that scar took him back in time and let him see himself as a little boy walking to school along a dirt path with his slate under his arm. One look at that scar and he knew that our eyes had already seen the yellow blossoms on the branches of plum trees at the front door of every house at New Year's. One look at that scar brought back to him the delicious aroma of caramelized fish with pepper, simmering in an earthen pot that sat directly on the coals. One look at that scar and our ears heard again the sound produced by the stem of a young bamboo as it sliced the air then lacerated the skin of our backsides. One look at that scar and our tropical roots, transplanted onto land covered with snow, emerged again. In one second we had seen our own ambivalence, our hybrid state: half this, half that, nothing at all and everything at once. A single mark on the skin and our entire shared history was spread out between two gas pumps in a station by a highway exit. He had concealed his scar under a midnight blue dragon. I couldn't see it with my naked eye. He had only to run his finger over my immodestly exhibited scar, however, and take my finger in his other hand and run it over the back of his dragon and immediately we experienced a moment of complicity, of communion.

I t was also a moment of communion when my
large extended family got together in upstate
New York to celebrate my grandmother's eighty-fifth
birthday. There were thirty-eight of us, gossiping,
giggling, getting on each other's nerves for two days.
I noticed then for the first time that I had the same
rounded thighs as Aunt Six and that the dress I had
on was similar to Aunt Eight's.

Aunt Eight is my big sister, the one who shared
with me the thrill of the word *goddess* that a man had
whispered in her ear when she was sitting, out of my
mother's sight, on the crossbar of his bicycle, encircled
by his arms. She is also the one who showed me how
to capture the pleasure of a passing desire, of an
ephemeral flattery, of a stolen moment.

When my cousin Sao Mai sat behind me and
embraced me for the cameras of her two sons,
Uncle Nine smiled. Uncle Nine knows me better
than I know myself because he bought me my
first novel, my first theatre ticket, my first visit to
a museum, my first journey.

S ao Mai became an important businesswoman, a public personality, a modern queen after she'd beaten dozens and dozens of eggs by hand—there were power failures five days out of seven in Saigon—to make birthday cakes that she sold to the new Communist leaders. Like an acrobat, she delivered her cakes by bicycle, zigzagging through other bicycles, avoiding the black smoke of motorcycles and the manholes with covers stolen. Today her cakes, and now also her ice cream, pastries, chocolate and coffee, are sold in every neighbourhood in the big cities, criss-crossing the country from south to north.

I am still the shadow of Sao Mai. But I like to be, because during my stay in Vietnam I was the shadow that danced around the bargaining tables to distract those with whom she was dealing while she deliberated. Because I was her shadow, she could confide in me her worries, her fears, her doubts, without compromising herself. Because I was her shadow, I was the only one who dared to enter her private life, which had been tightly sealed since the time when she sold "coffee" made from stale bread burned to a cinder then ground, on the sidewalk across from where she lived, ever since the windows of her house had been sold. Without asking permission, I relit the flames she thought had disappeared behind her now-massive facade. I cleared the way for frivolity by allowing her children to pelt each other with custard pies on my terrace, by putting them in a cardboard box full of confetti outside her room to wish her happy birthday when she woke up, by placing in her briefcase a red leather thong.

I like the red leather of the sofa in the cigar lounge
where I dare to strip naked in front of friends
and sometimes strangers, without their knowledge.
I recount bits of my past as if they were anecdotes or
comedy routines or amusing tales from far-off lands
featuring exotic landscapes, odd sound effects and
exaggerated characterizations. When I sit in that
smoky lounge, I forget that I'm one of the Asians
who lack the dehydrogenase enzyme for metabolizing
alcohol, I forget that I'm marked with a blue spot on
my backside, like the Inuit, like my sons, like all those
with Asian blood. I forget the mongoloid spot that
reveals the genetic memory because it vanished
during the early years of childhood, and my emotional
memory has been lost, dissolving, snarling with time.

That estrangement, that detachment, that distance allow me to buy, without any qualms and with full awareness of what I'm doing, a pair of shoes whose price in my native land would be enough to feed a family of five for one whole year. The salesperson just has to promise me, *You'll walk on air*, and I buy them. When we're able to float in the air, to separate ourselves from our roots—not only by crossing an ocean and two continents but by distancing ourselves from our condition as stateless refugees, from the empty space of an identity crisis—we can also laugh at whatever might have happened to my acrylic bracelet the colour of the gums on a dental plate, the bracelet my parents had turned into a survival kit by hiding all their diamonds in it. Who would have thought, after we avoided drowning, pirates, dysentery, that today the bracelet could be found perfectly intact, buried in a garbage dump? Who would have thought that burglars would steal from people living in an apartment as miserable as ours? Who would have imagined that thieves would saddle themselves with a ridiculous piece of jewellery made of pink plastic? All the members of my family are convinced that the burglars tossed it aside when they were sorting their haul. So maybe one day, millions of years from now, an archaeologist will wonder why diamonds were arranged in a circle and placed in

the ground. He may interpret it as a religious rite,
and the diamonds as a mysterious offering, like
all those gold taels discovered in amazing quantities
in the depths of the South China Sea.

R U

—

Absolutely no one will know the true story of the pink bracelet once the acrylic has decomposed into dust, once the years have accumulated in the thousands, in hundreds of strata, because after only thirty years I already recognize our old selves only through fragments, through scars, through glimmers of light.

In thirty years, Sao Mai resurfaced like a phoenix reborn from its ashes, like Vietnam from its iron curtain and my parents from the toilet bowls they had to scrub. Alone as much as together, all those individuals from my past have shaken the grime off their backs in order to spread their wings with plumage of red and gold, before thrusting themselves sharply towards the great blue space, decorating my children's sky, showing them that one horizon always hides another and it goes on like that to infinity, to the unspeakable beauty of renewal, to intangible rapture. As for me, it is true all the way to the possibility of this book, to the moment when my words glide across the curve of your lips, to the sheets of white paper that put up with my trail, or rather the trail of those who have walked before me, for me. I moved forward in the trace of their footsteps as in a waking dream where the scent of a newly blown poppy is no longer a perfume but a blossoming: where the deep red of a maple leaf in autumn is no longer a colour but a grace; where a country is no longer a place but a lullaby.

And also, where an outstretched hand is no longer a gesture but a moment of love, lasting until sleep, until waking, until everyday life.

KIM THÚY has worked as a seamstress, interpreter, lawyer and restaurant owner. *Ru* is her first book, has been published in 15 countries and received several awards, including the Governor General's Literary Award. Kim Thúy currently lives in Montreal, where she devotes herself to writing.

SHEILA FISCHMAN is the award-winning translator of some 150 contemporary novels from Quebec. In 2008 she was awarded the Molson Prize in the Arts. She is a Member of the Order of Canada and a chevalier de l'Ordre national du Québec. She lives in Montreal.

A NOTE ABOUT THE TYPE

The body of *Ru* has been set in Granjon, a modern
recutting of a typeface derived from the classic
letterforms of Claude Garamond (1480-1561).
It is named in honour of Robert Granjon, a successful
sixteenth-century French publisher, punch cutter
and founder, and a contemporary of Garamond.

Display text and drop caps are set in Linotype Didot.

READING GROUP GUIDE

These discussion questions are designed to enhance your group's conversation about *Ru*, an autobiographical novel based on the author's real-life experience as a Vietnamese émigré and how she found both her way—and her voice—after immigrating to Quebec.

ABOUT THIS BOOK

Ru is a fictionalized version of the author's own experience as a Vietnamese émigré. The narrator is ten when her family is forced to flee their home and luxurious lifestyle in Saigon because of the Communists. In vignettes that move between the past and present, the narrator tells of the Communist child inspectors who take up residence in their home and how her family flees in the dead of night by boat, taking only what is necessary with them and smuggling diamonds in vessels like shirt collars. They arrive in Malaysia, where her family is accepted by an overcrowded refugee camp that is plagued by flies and maggots and the narrator's mother insists that her daughter begin to learn English. Eventually, the family is able to settle in Quebec, where sponsors help them furnish their house, find clothes at the flea market, and acquire mattresses with actual fleas. It is only in Canada that the narrator, who spoke very little during her childhood, begins to open up, learning from teachers and friends the joy of language and song; it is these encounters that help the narrator realize she wishes to become a writer.

In addition to the concepts of identity and the American Dream, woven throughout the novel are the narrator's stories of her immediate and extended family. Readers learn about the narrator's mother, the strict authoritarian who only learned to be herself when she took up dancing in her mid-fifties. Then there is her father, who has only ever lived in the present and who teaches his daughter to let go of any attachment to the past. There is her cousin Sao Mai, whom she shadows throughout their childhood and who speaks on the narrator's behalf but also bosses her around. There is the narrator's Uncle Two, her mother's eldest brother, who was a member of parliament, loved the arts, was popular with many, and to whom the narrator reads poetry on his deathbed. There is the her paternal grandfather, who had stopped speaking after his stroke, who lies on the ebony daybed in his white pajamas all day, and whose blue supper bowls have been passed down to the narrator to use for her own sons, Pascal and Henri, who is autistic. The narrator includes stories of becoming a mother to her two boys and how her experience with motherhood has taught her the true meaning of love and belonging.

1. The novel's title, *Ru*, has different meanings in both the author's native and adoptive languages: in Vietnamese, *ru* is a lullaby; in French, a stream. How do these two different meanings play out during the course of the book?

2. Thúy has chosen to tell her story in short vignettes, often linked by subject rather than chronology. What do you think her reasoning might be for choosing this form over a more traditional narrative arc?

3. The narrator reveals in the first pages of *Ru* that her name is a variation of her mother's, that she was supposed to be her mother's extension and sequel, but that this role ended when she was ten years old (2). Why and how does her relationship to her mother change?

4. The narrator describes herself in childhood as being her cousin Sao Mai's "shadow" (18). What does she mean? What are some of the other times in her life when she feels like a shadow?

5. About the Communist child inspectors living in her family's home, the narrator writes: "We no

longer knew if they were enemies or victims, if we loved or hated them, if we feared or pitied them. And they no longer knew if they had freed us from the Americans, or, on the contrary, if we had freed them from the jungle of Vietnam" (32). How does the narrator's up-is-down-and-down-is-up war experience continue to color her views toward her homeland and its people throughout the course of her life?

6. Constant movement is one of *Ru*'s themes. At one point, the narrator writes, "I never leave a place with more than one suitcase . . . Nothing else can become truly mine" (100). Why do you think she believes this? Do you think it is true for her?

7. In, Vietnamese, the narrator tells us, there are different words for different ways of loving (96). But the narrator says it is her children who define for her what it means simply "to love" (102). How do you think her love for her children is different from what she feels for her parents, relatives, or lovers?

8. The narrator describes an incident at restaurant school in Hanoi when a waiter reminded her that she "no longer had the right to declare that [she] was Vietnamese because [she] no longer

had their fragility, their uncertainty, their fears"
(78). The narrator seems to believe he was right;
do you?

9. Music appears throughout the book in various
   forms and situations: the music the narrator's
   father plays on the piano to corrupt the child
   inspectors; the Fame theme song Johanne
   teaches her to sing; the music her middle-aged
   mother dances to in her weekly dance classes;
   the melodies the strolling merchants sing while
   advertising their basket wares. What is music's
   importance in *Ru*?

10. The American Dream plays an integral role in
    the narrator's life and her search for meaning,
    and she references it often during the novel.
    What is her version of the American Dream?
    Do you think she attains it?

11. The narrator speaks of the Vietnamese women
    permanently hunched by the weight of their
    grief (39). To what extent do you think she
    identifies with those women?

12. Many aspects of this novel are clearly autobio-
    graphical, but the author classifies it as fiction.
    Why do you think Thúy chose to write the
    book she did, rather than a straight memoir?

SUGGESTED READING

Rhea Tregebov, *The Knife Sharpener's Bell*; Jean Kwok, *Girl in Translation*; Katherine Boo, *Behind the Beautiful Forevers*; Anthony Shadid, *House of Stone*; William Saroyan, *My Name Is Aram*; Robert Trando, *Letters of a Vietnamese Émigré*; John Bul Dau, *God Grew Tired of Us*; Lac Su, *I Love You's Are for White People*; Sopheap Ly, M.D., *No Dream Beyond My Reach*; Chanrithy Him, *When Broken Glass Floats*; Juliet Lac, *Blossoms on the Wind*; Le Ly Hayslip, *When Heaven and Earth Changed Places* and *Child of War, Woman of Peace*; Andrew X. Pham, *The Eaves of Heaven*